ABOUT

Barbara Cartland, the world
who is also an historian, pla
and television personality, ha
sold over 500 million copies

She has also had many h
written four autobiographies as well as the biographies of her
mother and that of her brother, Ronald Cartland, who was the
first Member of Parliament to be killed in the last war. This
book has a preface by Sir Winston Churchill and has just been
republished with an introduction by the late Sir Arthur Bryant.

Love at the Helm, a novel written with the help and inspiration
of the late Earl Mountbatten of Burma, Great Uncle of His
Royal Highness The Prince of Wales, is being sold for the
Mountbatten Memorial Trust.

She has broken the world record for the last thirteen years
by writing an average of twenty-three books a year. In the
Guiness Book of Records she is listed as the world's top-selling
author.

Miss Cartland in 1978 sang an Album of Love Songs with the
Royal Philharmonic orchestra.

In private life Barbara Cartland, who is a Dame of Grace of
the Order of St. John of Jerusalem, Chairman of the St. John
Council in Hertfordshire and Deputy President of the St. John
Ambulance Brigade, has fought for better conditions and salar-
ies for Midwives and Nurses.

She championed the cause for the Elderly in 1956 invoking
a Government Enquiry into the "Housing Conditions of Old
People".

In 1962 she had the Law of England changed so that Local
Authorities had to provide camps for their own Gypsies. This
has meant that since then thousands and thousands of Gypsy
children have been able to go to School which they had never
been able to do in the past, as their caravans were moved every
twenty-four hours by the Police.

There are now fourteen camps in Hertfordshire and Barbara

Cartland has her own Romany Gypsy Camp called Barbaraville by the Gypsies.

Her designs "Decorating with Love" are being sold all over the U.S.A. and the National Home Fashions League made her, in 1981, "Woman of Achievement".

Barbara Cartland's book *Getting Older, Growing Younger* has been published in Great Britain and the U.S.A. and her fifth Cookery Book, *The Romance of Food*, is now being used by the House of Commons.

In 1984 she received at Kennedy Airport, America's Bishop Wright Air Industry Award for her contribution to the development of aviation. In 1931 she and two R.A.F. Officers thought of, and carried the first aeroplane-towed glider air-mail.

During the War she was Chief Lady Welfare Officer in Bedfordshire looking after 20,000 Service men and women. She thought of having a pool of Wedding Dresses at the War Office so a Service Bride could hire a gown for the day.

She bought 1,000 secondhand gowns without coupons for the A.T.S., the W.A.A.F.s and the W.R.N.S. In 1945 Barbara Cartland received the Certificate of Merit from Eastern Command.

In 1964 Barbara Cartland founded the National Association for Health of which she is the President, as a front for all the Health Stores and for any product made as alternative medicine.

This has now a £500,000,000 turnover a year, with one third going in export.

In January 1988 she received "La Medaille de Vermeil de la Ville de Paris", (the Gold Medal of Paris). This is the highest award to be given by the City of Paris for ACHIEVEMENT – 25 million books sold in France.

In March 1988 Barbara Cartland was asked by the Indian Government to open their Health Resort outside Delhi. This is almost the largest Health Resort in the world.

Barbara Cartland was received with great enthusiasm by her fans, who also fêted her at a Reception in the city and she received the gift of an embossed plate from the Government.

REAL LOVE OR FAKE

The Marquis of Kyneston is furious when the Beauty with whom he is having a passionate *affaire de coeur* is unfaithful to him and even argues when he unexpectedly calls on his mistress and finds she has another lover in the house with which he had provided her.

He decides he hates all women and goes off in his yacht to Amsterdam to buy Dutch pictures for a Collection which is already famous.

How a very beautiful young girl called Lela tries to sell him the sketch Johann Vermeer did for his portrait *Head of a Girl*; how the Marquis rescues her from being assaulted by the unscrupulous son of her Aunt, how because she is English he offers to take her home and how because of an accident the Marquis falls hopelessly in love is told in this 423rd book by Barbara Cartland.

by the same author in Pan

THE LADY AND THE HIGHWAYMAN
A HAZARD OF HEARTS
A CHIEFTAIN FINDS LOVE
A KNIGHT IN PARIS
LOVE AT FIRST SIGHT
THE LOVELY LIAR
THE NECKLACE OF LOVE
PARADISE IN PENANG
THE PASSIONATE PRINCESS
REVENGE IS SWEET
SOLITA AND THE SPIES
THE TAMING OF A TIGRESS
KISS FROM A STRANGER

BARBARA CARTLAND

REAL LOVE
OR FAKE

Pan Original
Pan Books London, Sydney and Auckland

First published 1990 by Pan Books Ltd,
Cavaye Place, London SW10 9PG
9 8 7 6 5 4 3 2 1
© Cartland Promotions 1990
ISBN 0 330 31203 0
Phototypeset by Input Typesetting Ltd, London
Printed and bound in Great Britain by
Courier International Ltd, Tiptree, Essex

AUTHOR'S NOTE

When I was in Amsterdam I found the portraits in the Rijksmuseum were beautifully painted by Rubens and Rembrandt but the Dutch appear never to have had their portraits done until they were old and Burgomasters.

It is therefore a joy to see in the Mauritshuis – *Head of a Girl* by Johannes Vermeer – he was one of Holland's brilliant seventeenth-century painters whose style was copied so cleverly in modern times by a man called Tom Keating.

After the Second World War the paintings General Goebbels had stolen from all European countries were returned and no one would believe the Vermeers were not genuine until Keating confessed he had painted them.

The Head of a Girl was acquired in 1882 for only two guilders thirty cents by Des Tombe a collector, and was left to the Mauritshuis in 1903.

I loved the canals in Amsterdam with the exquisite old houses which I have described in this novel. It is a City of a Thousand and One bridges.

Chapter One
1903

The Marquis of Kyneston came into London in a good temper.

He was driving his Four-in-Hand, and his team of chestnuts was the admiration of everybody he passed on the street.

He felt he had to describe to somebody his success in what had been one of the most difficult races for which he had ever entered a horse.

He therefore drew up outside White's Club and handed the reins to his groom.

"Take the horses home, James," he said, "and send back my closed carriage. I will be ready to leave in under an hour."

"Very good, M'Lord."

The Marquis walked into the Club with a swagger.

He had not only won an outstanding race, but he had also broken his own record for returning to London.

There were, he knew, many of his friends who now preferred to travel by train or, even more adventurous, in the new motorcars which had an inconvenient habit of breaking down after a few miles.

He, however, was determined to keep his horses.

There were a number of other men like himself who said that if horseflesh was doomed, they were too.

He walked into the Morning Room to find, as he expected, a number of his friends congregated there.

He saw first Willy Melivale who was one of his closest contemporaries, and with whom he had been at school.

He walked to the far end of the room where Willy was sitting to find there was a chair empty beside him.

"Hello, Carew!" Willy exclaimed, "You need not tell me! I know by your face that you have won again."

"I have!" the Marquis replied. "I only wish you had been there. It was such a close finish that both Crayford and I held our breath!"

"But actually you were the winner!" Willy said with just a touch of sarcasm in his voice.

"Yes, I won!" the Marquis said with satisfaction.

He ordered himself a drink, then sat back comfortably in the leather armchair, thinking it had been one of the best days he could remember.

"What are you doing tonight?" Willy asked. "I thought we might dine together."

There was a moment's pause. Then the Marquis replied:

"I would have liked that, but unfortunately I am engaged."

He thought as he spoke that to be with Daphne Burton as he intended would be a fitting climax to his triumph on the race-course.

He had met Lady Burton four weeks ago for the first time.

Having watched her at a large dinner-party at Apsley House, he thought she was without exception one of the most attractive women he had ever seen.

There was something fascinating about her that was more important than mere beauty.

He was not surprised when the gentlemen joined the ladies in the Drawing-Room to find her at his side.

"I have heard so much about you, My Lord," she said in a soft, caressing voice.

"All, I hope, to my advantage!" the Marquis remarked.

He was amused by the questioning look in her dark eyes and the touch of mockery on her perfect lips as she replied:

"But, of course! How could it be anything else?"

He laughed, and he knew that they were both thinking that while he was distinguished in many ways, his love-affairs occupied the minds and tongues of the gossips.

"Heaven knows, I try to be discreet!" he told himself.

Unfortunately however, he was too important and too successful for both men and women not to talk about him.

The King had set the fashion when he was the Prince of Wales of flaunting his love-affairs.

It was difficult for the Marquis to do anything different.

He was however, apart from being an exceptional horseman, a conscientious Landlord, giving much of his time and attention to his estates.

He was at the moment attending in great detail to his ancestral home Kyne in Huntingfordshire.

It was a magnificent example of Palladian architecture.

Later generations had made few modern improvements, and had neglected the State Rooms until now they were in urgent need of redecoration.

The Marquis had also tried to buy back some of the Georgian furniture which had been replaced with what he considered 'Victorian horrors' at the beginning of the Queen's long reign.

One important step was to enlarge the Picture Gallery.

He had added to it a number of paintings by artists who had not been appreciated by his forebears.

He had recently acquired a painting of Venus which had delighted him until he saw Lady Burton and decided that she would have been a more worthy applicant for the title.

He pursued her at first somewhat languidly, then more

11

determinedly, as he was finding it difficult to see her on her own.

"My husband is very jealous," she told him, "and you will therefore understand that, although I want to see you, it would be a mistake."

"What do you mean – a mistake?" the Marquis had demanded, and now he felt even more ardent than before.

There had been snatched moments in the afternoons, which he had always thought, even though it was fashionable, a tiresome time to make love.

When they had met at an house party given by the Earl of Doncaster, Lord Burton had been with his wife, and was obviously very possessive about her.

The Marquis had then thought despairingly that he would have to give up the chase.

Unexpectedly Daphne Burton had told him two days ago that her husband was going to Paris.

"He will be away from Wednesday until Friday," she said.

The Marquis waited.

"I thought," Lady Burton went on, "that perhaps you would dine with me on Thursday night, just a small party."

It was not what she said but the look in her eyes which told the Marquis exactly what was intended.

They would dine conventionally with friends and he would linger after they had left, being the last to go.

"You know I will be looking forward to it," he said in his deep voice.

"So shall . . I," she whispered.

There was no chance to say any more, but the Marquis had found on the following two days his thoughts quite frequently going towards Thursday evening.

He was certain that Daphne Burton would be everything a man could desire in a woman – feminine, yielding, fiery and very exciting.

12

"It is just my good luck that Henry Burton should go to Paris when everybody else is in London for the Season, and unlikely to go anywhere else," he told himself.

At the same time, he knew he would have enjoyed dining with Willy, when he could tell him every detail of the race, and they could discuss what horses he should enter for Ascot.

Then as he was thinking about it, Willy asked:

"Are you dining with Daphne Burton tonight?"

"Yes, I am," the Marquis replied, "and I suppose you too are a guest?"

"No," Willy answered, "I have not been invited!"

There was something in the way he spoke which made the Marquis look at him curiously.

He knew Willy so well.

They had been so close all their lives that it was difficult for either of them to keep secrets from the other.

Now the Marquis was perceptively aware that Willy was not looking at him, but turning something over in his mind.

He had no idea what it could be, because even with such a close friend as Willy he never discussed his love-affairs.

He thought therefore that what was worrying him could not concern Daphne Burton.

He finished his drink and was just about to look at the time when Willy said:

"I saw Henry Burton this afternoon!"

The Marquis was suddenly still.

"You saw Henry Burton?" he repeated. "But that is impossible! He is in Paris!"

"I saw him when I was driving back from Ranelagh," Willy said. "I took a wrong turning somewhere in the suburbs and distinctly saw him going into what appeared to me to be a rather sleazy-looking hotel."

The Marquis was staring at his friend incredulously.

13

"You are quite sure it was Burton?"

Willy nodded.

Then after a silence he said:

"I would not otherwise have told you, but Daron Haughton lost a lot of money to him about twelve months ago."

"Daron Haughton?" the Marquis asked.

"He met the Burtons in the country," Willy explained.

The Marquis remembered Daphne Burton telling him that was the reason why they had not met before.

She had been living in the country owing to being in mourning for her Mother.

Lord Haughton was, the Marquis knew, a very rich man to whom it would not have mattered particularly to lose money.

But it seemed strange that Burton, whom he knew to be hard up, should have been the recipient of it.

He sat back in his chair and said in a voice which his friend knew could be very authoritative:

"You had better tell me the whole story, Willy."

"Very well," Willy said lowering his voice. "It is quite simple. Burton came home unexpectedly, and Haughton paid up!"

The Marquis's lips tightened and without saying any more he rose and walked towards the door.

Willy watched him go, then he sighed and signalled to a Club steward to bring him another drink.

The Marquis's carriage was just pulling up outside the Club as he walked down the steps.

As he got into it the expression on his face was very different from what it had been when he arrived.

When he was in a rage he did not lose his temper in the way most men did, becoming aggressive, shouting or swearing, and in many cases having a rush of blood to the head.

14

Instead, the Marquis became icily calm.

Those who knew him well found his silences more intimidating than anything anybody else could have said.

As he walked through the front door of his house in Park Lane his footmen, all over six foot, stood more stiffly to attention than usual.

The Butler's voice was very respectful as he asked if His Lordship had any orders for the evening.

The Marquis considered for a moment.

Then he said: "My carriage at seven-thirty!" and walked up the stairs.

He was silent while his valet helped him undress.

After he had stayed in his bath for a long time, he dressed himself in his elegant evening clothes.

He was thinking bitterly as he did so how much he had looked forward to this evening.

"Perhaps it is just a mistake," he thought.

Then he knew that Willy would not have said he had seen Burton unless he had been absolutely certain of it.

The Marquis had been pursued all his life by women who had found him irresistible from the time he left School.

He was in fact a very handsome man.

Because he was an exceptional rider, and indulged in every possible form of outdoor sport, he had an athletic figure of which he was justly proud.

He drank very little compared to his friends.

He was a deliberately small eater compared to the King and those who had surrounded him at Marlborough House, and now at Buckingham Palace.

The Marquis could not remember a time when there had not been women eulogising over him, and telling him he looked like a Greek god.

It was something he was only too willing to believe.

He found it difficult to accept that of all the women on

whom he had bestowed his favours Daphne Burton should be interested in him simply because he was rich.

He knew exactly how a man like him could be trapped if a husband and wife were collaborating and playing their cards cleverly.

If Willy was right, Daphne's plans for tonight were for her other guests to leave early while he stayed behind.

She would take him up to her bedroom.

They would be in bed when the door would open and Henry Burton would rush in.

Daphne would scream in horror while he would stare at her as if he could hardly believe his eyes.

There would then be a scene with accusations and recriminations.

Burton would aver that having caught them red-handed he would immediately sue for divorce.

Daphne would plead with him pathetically to spare her the scandal and ostracism that would ensue.

This, the Marquis knew, would be his cue to intervene.

To save himself, and of course the woman whose reputation he had ruined, he would be expected to offer the affronted husband a large sum of money to assuage her pride and the slur on his name.

It would all take time and would be extremely humiliating.

He would be naked, while Burton was fully dressed in the clothes in which he was supposed to have travelled from Paris.

It was the sort of situation which would make a good melodrama at the Playhouse, but not so funny when one was actively involved.

He could see all too clearly how Haughton had been caught, with nothing he could do in the circumstances but pay whatever Burton demanded.

He would be in the same predicament, except that as

he was richer than Lord Haughton he would find the settlement more expensive.

"How can I possibly have been such a fool?" he asked himself.

He thought now that he might have guessed that the Burtons were extremely hard up.

They had doubtless already spent most of what they had obtained from Daron Haughton by the time they had encountered him.

Burton enjoyed gambling, while his wife wished to move in the Social World in a way that would inevitably incur heavy expenditure.

Their house was not large, but it was in fashionable Mayfair.

They had a carriage and horses, and the Marquis had heard that Burton had hunted with the Leicester pack of hounds last winter.

There was no doubt that they would be running short of money by this time.

Who better to supply them with more than himself?

His lips were set in a hard line as he walked down the stairs just before seven-thirty to where the Butler was waiting with his evening-cloak lined with red satin.

One footman handed him his top hat, another his cane, and a third his gloves.

Without speaking he went out through the front door and stepped into the carriage.

A footman in the Kyneston livery was holding open the door.

Another footman placed a lined rug over his knees and the carriage moved off.

It was not far to the Burtons' house which was in one of the narrower streets a short way from Shepherd Market.

As he entered the house he noticed for the first time that the carpets in the hall were slightly threadbare.

The arrangement of flowers half-way up the stairs was not of the most expensive Malmaison carnations.

As the Butler opened the door to the Drawing-Room and announced his name the Marquis forced a smile to his lips.

"The Marquis of Kyneston, M'Lady!"

Daphne Burton turned from the man to whom she was talking with a little cry of delight.

She moved towards the Marquis with a grace which had made him think she floated over the ground.

There was an expression of pleasure in her eyes and on her fascinating face which he could not believe was assumed.

"I am so glad to see you," she said softly as he took her hand and felt her fingers tighten on his.

She introduced her other guests who were, as the Marquis had expected, quite elderly.

There was one man who had retired several years ago, having been a distinguished Diplomat, with his wife, and another couple, neither of whom would ever see sixty again.

It was almost, he thought as he went in to dinner, as if he was reading a chapter from a book he had read before, and knew exactly what would happen next.

The dinner was good, although it did not compare with what his Chefs produced at any of his own houses.

The wine was drinkable, but not, as he knew, particularly expensive.

The conversation would have been dull except for the expression in his hostess's eyes when she looked at him and the manner in which she touched him almost accidentally with her fingers.

There was, he thought, a deliberate *double entendre* in many of the things she said to him.

When the gentlemen left the Dining Room, the Marquis was not surprised when the elderly Diplomat said:

"Will you forgive us, My Lord, if we leave early? My wife is not in good health, and we are both growing too old to enjoy late nights."

"I am sure you are wise," the Marquis said conventionally.

"I am careful, which is very much the same thing," the ageing Diplomat replied.

The Marquis thought that the wisdom of taking care applied to him also.

As the two couples left together he waited until they had proceeded down the stairs and were putting on their coats in the hall.

Then he said quietly:

"I too must be on my way."

"You are – leaving?"

There was no doubt of the astonishment in Daphne Burton's voice and the expression of consternation on her face.

She looked attractive and so genuinely concerned.

It flashed through the Marquis's mind that Willy had been mistaken and that she was really attracted to him as a man.

She had certainly seemed to be so all the time they were next to each other at the dinner table.

He did not speak and after a moment she said hesitatingly:

"I . . I thought . . I believed . . that you and I could be . . together as I have wanted to be for . . so long."

"That is what I too had hoped," the Marquis replied, "but I hear that your husband is back from Paris, so of course there is now no question of our being alone."

He was watching her very carefully as he spoke.

He knew by the surprised flicker of her eyes and the way she drew in her breath that Willy had been right.

There was just too long a pause before she exclaimed:

19

"Henry – back? What are you saying? He is not expected until tomorrow."

"I think you are mistaken," the Marquis said. "Goodnight, and I must thank you for a most enjoyable dinner."

He raised her hand perfunctorily to his lips, and while she was still speechless at what had happened, he went from the room.

He was down the stairs and into the hall as the last of the other guests were passing through the front door.

His carriage was waiting and as he drove away he thought he had won again, but this time it was a hollow victory.

He had been saved by a hair's breadth from being made a fool of, and it was something he would never forget.

Then he realised the carriage was taking him home.

He decided he could not bear to go to bed so early to think of Daphne Burton and how easily she had deceived him.

He put out his cane to tap in the glass window behind the coachman and the horses came to a standstill.

The footman then got down from the box and opened the door.

The Marquis gave him an address and the footman climbed back up onto the box again.

He had for some time been without a mistress, who was as much a normal part of a rich man's possessions as his horses.

Then two months ago he had, after some deliberation installed a very attractive Gaiety Girl in a pleasant house in St. John's Wood.

Dolly Leslie was in *The Toreador*, which was to be the last Show to take place at the old Gaiety Theatre.

Then it was to be pulled down and a new Gaiety Theatre to be opened in October.

This would be the passing of one of the most famous

Theatres ever to entrance the populace. It was in fact a part of English history.

The old streets around it that went back to Tudor times were also to be pulled down, and London was changing.

One thing fortunately had not changed for a long time, and that was the beauty of the Gaiety Girls, and the fact that they were unique.

They had brought to London something entirely new which had not been known before.

Lovely as goddesses, the Gaiety Girls floated through the Theatre with a grace and beauty that was all their own.

George Edwards had become known as the best picker of feminine charm the world had ever known.

From 1868 onwards the Gaiety Shows had shone, glittered and entranced with an irresistible magic, and all London flocked to them.

The Marquis would have been inhuman if he had been impervious, as no man was, to their charm.

But he thought Dolly Leslie was even more magnetic than the other girls the moment she appeared on the stage.

It had not been hard to convince her that she would find it impossible to discover another man so attractive or so generous as himself.

At least three nights a week when he was in London he sat in his box at the Theatre enjoying the Shows, watching Dolly.

He then took her out to supper at Romano's.

After that they would go back to the house he had made attractive not only for Dolly but also for himself.

He had finished it with the same concentration he gave to his large houses.

He had installed a bathroom which was sensational, and stocked the cellar.

Not surprisingly he also chose the servants as he chose

everything else, so that when he stayed the night with Dolly he was as comfortable as if he was in his house in Park Lane.

When he was with her on Tuesday he had told her that he would not be seeing her again that week.

On Wednesday he was going to the races, and would stay the night with friends in the country.

On Thursday he was dining out, and on Friday he intended to go to Kyne for the weekend.

Dolly said how she would miss him.

He had consoled her by giving her a very expensive diamond bracelet which he had bought that afternoon in Bond Street.

She thanked him very prettily, and he told himself when he left her that it would be difficult for any man to find a more enchanting mistress.

It took some time for the carriage to reach St. John's Wood.

The Marquis calculated that Dolly would have been home from the Theatre for nearly two hours.

She would have driven from the Stage Door in the carriage he had given her, drawn by a horse he had bought at Tattersall's.

She would undoubtedly be thrilled to see him, and because it was a surprise she would be even more ardent than usual.

He told himself that in future he would stick to girls like Dolly and be extremely wary of embarking again on any *affaire de coeur* with a woman of his own class.

It was in fact the King, when he was Prince of Wales, who had made it possible for a Gentleman to have affairs with women who could be described as 'Ladies'.

Before that there had been a rigid distinction between a mistress and a Lady.

Even one breath of scandal in the Social World meant

22

that the woman concerned was ostracised by all her friends.

To all intents and purposes she ceased to exist.

The Prince of Wales however had moved from Lily Langtry to the alluring Lady Brook with whom he was genuinely in love.

He continued through numerous *social boudoirs* until at the moment he was entranced by the fascinating Mrs. Grenville.

She was accepted from the very beginning of their affair by Princess Alexandra.

It was all such a reversal of anything that had happened in the past that it was hard for many of the puritanical Dowagers to believe what they heard.

Now, because he felt angry and bitter, the Marquis told himself they were right.

He would take care in the future to confine himself to a mistress.

She would be faithful to him for as long as he was her Protector, and the social ladies could remain with their husbands.

He only hoped as his carriage rolled on that Henry Burton and his wife were asking themselves how it was possible for him to have become aware of what they had planned.

At the same time, it was small consolation to think that it was only due to Willy that he was not at this very moment being ignominiously humiliated without having any defence.

The carriage turned in at the small 'In-and-Out' drive in front of the Villa.

Then as the horses came to an abrupt standstill the Marquis was aware there was another carriage in front blocking the entrance to the door.

For a moment he thought it must be his own carriage which had brought Dolly back from the Theatre.

Then he realised it was long after midnight.

By this time the coachman, unless she had been somewhere else first, would have taken it round to the Mews at the back of the house.

Curious to know what had happened, he opened the carriage door himself and stepped out.

He walked across the grass to approach the carriage which he could now see was drawn, unlike his own, by only one horse.

There was a coachman on the box sitting in such a relaxed attitude that it was obvious he expected to have a long wait.

Then as the Marquis looked at the man an idea flashed through his mind.

He drew nearer to the carriage to stare at the crest which was painted on the door.

One look at it told him what he had already begun to suspect, and he knew the owner was inside with Dolly.

It was a young Peer who had been pursuing her before he appeared.

She had told him that she found Lord Brora amusing and had allowed him to take her to Romano's on several occasions.

But His Lordship was not over-endowed with this world's goods, and Dolly had said quite frankly that he could not afford her.

The Marquis had not been particularly interested.

Except he had a feeling of jubilation at having "pipped another man at the post", making sure that, like his horses, he came in first.

Now as he stared at Lord Brora's crest he told himself furiously that, if he was correct in his suspicions, then Dolly was breaking all the rules of the game.

It was in fact understood that a man's mistress, if he was generous towards her, was faithful to him so long as he paid the way.

24

Most especially if he provided her with a house.

To make quite certain that in thinking the worst he was not mistaken, the Marquis passed the carriage, climbed up the two steps to the front door and opened it with his key.

The structure of the house was very simple.

There was a long Sitting-Room on one side with a bedroom directly above it.

On the other side of the hall there was a small Dining-Room and a kitchen behind it.

Above there was another bedroom which the Marquis had divided into a dressing-room and a bathroom.

The hall was in darkness, and he opened the door into the Sitting-Room to find that all the lights had been extinguished.

As he stood there he heard from the room above the sound of voices, then a light laugh.

He stood for a moment as if turned to stone.

Then with the same icy calm with which he had started the evening, he walked slowly out of the house, shutting the door behind him, and climbed back into his carriage.

The coachman was already backing the horses out into the road, and as the footman jumped down to open the carriage-door the Marquis said briefly:

"Home!"

He had been deceived not once by a woman but twice, and that was something he vowed would never occur again.

It was certainly something he had never experienced before.

He could hardly believe it possible that he, of all people, should be treated so treacherously, not only by Daphne Burton, but also by his mistress.

He had, he felt, been exceedingly generous towards Dolly, who he had believed had a real affection for him.

That she had failed him was just as humiliating as if he had been found naked in bed by Burton.

"Damn them both!" he swore to himself beneath his breath. "And damn all women for being treacherous and untrustworthy!"

As he drove on the Marquis told himself that never again would he believe anything any woman said to him.

As he arrived home the night-footman opened the door and he walked past him without speaking.

He went up to his bedroom and rang for his valet.

He seemed surprised to see him back so early, but was too tactful to remark upon it.

He helped the Marquis undress, then taking his evening-clothes over his arm, he went to the door saying before he left:

"Goodnight, M'Lord!"

The Marquis did not reply, he merely blew out the candles to lie thinking furiously he was completely disillusioned.

At the same time, he had no intention of letting anybody know about it.

Tomorrow his Secretary would be told to pay Dolly off and order her to leave the house as soon as possible.

Regrettably, he thought, he would not therefore be able to attend the last night at the Gaiety Theatre before it closed.

To do so would inevitably make his friends, who would expect to see him afterwards with Dolly at Romano's, ask questions.

Willy would also be curious, although he would not ask what had happened tonight when he had dined with Daphne Burton.

Because he was still smarting at the way he had been treated, the Marquis had no wish to be in a defensive position.

Nor did he wish to let people suspect for one moment that he was not his ordinary victorious self.

He knew he could not bear to have anybody pity him or for that matter to have Lord Brora and Dolly talking about what had happened.

They would of course know.

Lord Brora's coachman would certainly tell him that the Marquis had arrived, walked into the house and immediately come out again.

There would then be no doubt about it when Dolly received her Notice to Quit.

He wished almost childishly that he had not on Tuesday given her a bracelet that had cost a considerable amount of money and was far better than any of the other jewels she owned.

Then he told himself he must go away.

The only answer to his problems was to disappear where no one could ask him questions and no one would suspect that he had been made to look a fool by two women.

He realised that any suspicion of the truth would create a story that would fly around London, and doubtless amuse the King.

His Majesty had always enjoyed tittle-tattle, especially if it concerned a woman, or in this case, two of them!

"I will have to go away," the Marquis thought.

Then he had an idea.

The last time the King had visited Kyne he had remarked when he visited the Picture Gallery:

"I see, Kyneston, that you are rather short of Dutch pictures. I know you have always admired those at Buckingham Palace that were bought by George IV, and I have always been grateful that he had the sense to acquire them when no one else was interested.

"You are quite right, Sir," the Marquis had replied, "and I will look out for some of the Dutch Masters."

"They are not as pretty as the French," the King said, "and that certainly applies to their women! But they are good value, and I have always been an admirer of Cuyp."

"So have I, Sir," the Marquis replied.

Now as the conversation came into his mind, he thought it was a message from the gods when he most needed their help.

There was sure to be a sale of good pictures of some sort taking place in Amsterdam.

No one would be surprised if he went there to see what he could add to his collection.

He gave a sigh of relief.

At the last moment, when he had felt he was drowning, he had been thrown a lifeline.

He would leave London tomorrow.

Chapter Two

Lela walked out through the front door and looked up at the sun coming through the trees.

"It is a lovely day, Nanny," she said with a lilt in her voice.

"It'll be hot later," Nanny said, as if she must find fault with something.

Lela was not listening.

She was thinking how exciting it was to be in Holland and see the beauty of the Hague around her.

The red brick houses with their strange gables were a delight every time she looked at them.

She thought that nothing could be more exciting than that at this moment she was going to the Mauritshuis Museum.

She walked on a little way until almost without thinking she spoke her thoughts aloud.

"I am sure Step-Papa will not find me here!"

"I hope not, Miss Lela!" Nanny replied.

Lela gave a little shiver.

Every night she prayed fervently that it would never enter her Stepfather's mind that she had crossed the North Sea and come to Holland.

She could remember only too vividly how horrified she had been when she returned home a month ago after having been away for nearly three years.

She had been excited when she left her school in Florence at the idea of seeing England again.

Although she knew it would bring back all too vividly the agony of losing her mother.

But she had thought there would be compensations in being back in her own country.

She had however been bitterly disillusioned.

When her father had been killed in the last year of the Boer War her mother's world had fallen to pieces.

She had been so overwhelmingly in love with her tall, handsome husband.

She had in fact loved him passionately from the first moment she had seen him.

It was not surprising, because Captain Harry Cavendish was not only exceedingly good-looking, but had a charm which was irresistible both to men and women.

As soon as Mildred Warde saw him, she had found it impossible to find any other man in the Regiment attractive.

As Harry thought the same about her, it was only a question of time before they were married.

They were so much in love that the whole room seemed to light up when they were together.

But of course nothing is ever perfect, and the parents on both sides asked what they were going to live on.

Harry had a small allowance from his father besides his pay as a soldier, and Mildred had what was little more than "pin money".

Harry however swept every objection aside.

After they were married they were too happy to notice that their surroundings were not as luxurious as they might have wished.

They had settled down in a small house in the country and were content with their horses and their child, a daughter.

Then the Boer War started and Harry, who was on the the Reserve, was called up immediately.

As was to be expected, he distinguished himself.

After being mentioned in dispatches several times he was awarded the Victoria Cross, the supreme decoration for valour.

Mildred was very proud.

At the same time she was desperately afraid for her husband because he was in danger.

Her anguish was proved only too true, when a few months later he was killed.

It took a little time, because she was grief-stricken, to realise that with Harry's death she had not only lost him, but also her own and Lela's means of survival.

She was wondering what she could do, having no wish to encumber her family with two poor relations, when Sir Robert Lawson came into her life.

A much older man, nearing forty, he had been a widower for over ten years, and had for some time vaguely contemplated the idea of marrying again.

When he met Mildred Cavendish he knew she was everything he had ever sought in a woman, and without exception the most beautiful person he had ever seen.

It took him six months to persuade her to marry him.

It was only when it be came a choice between marrying Sir Robert, who was very rich, or begging her relatives, who were not well off, to support her, that Mildred agreed.

At the last moment she thought that loving Harry as she had it would be impossible to allow any other man to touch her.

Yet because Sir Robert was older, and at the same time extremely generous, she felt it was her duty to provide for Lela, and not be an encumbrance on anybody else.

They moved to his very comfortable house in Oxfordshire.

Lela, who was now fourteen years of age, found his horses, which were superb, a new excitement.

If Lady Lawson wanted to be compensated for what she had done, it was to see Lela's face, which was so like her own, alight with joy and her eyes shining as she came in from riding.

"I jumped higher today, Mama, than I ever have jumped before!" she would announce proudly.

Her mother would put her arms around her as she said gently:

"I know how proud your father would be of you. He was a magnificent rider, and won all the Point-to-Points and Steeplechases at home!"

It was impossible, however comfortable they might now be, not to think of the little Manor House where they had been so happy.

But it was a mistake to live in the past, and Mildred made a tremendous effort to please Sir Robert.

She knew he was proud of her.

She knew too that he enjoyed the parties at which she sat looking exceedingly lovely at the end of the table wearing the jewels with which he festooned her.

Some of the men who came to the house she did not like.

Gradually she persuaded Sir Robert to entertain more distinguished County people, of whom there were quite a number living in their neighbourhood.

They also went to London where they met members of the Political World which gave him an insight into a subject about which he had not thought before.

Then when Lela was fifteen her mother suggested to Sir Robert that she should go to a finishing School in Florence.

"She should come out in the Season of 1902," she said, "and I want her to be better educated and more intelligent than debutantes usually are."

He had laughed and said:

"Most men will not be looking for brains in anything as beautiful as Lela, who is exactly like you."

"All the same, I want her to be intelligent," Lady Lawson persisted.

Good-humouredly Sir Robert agreed, paying a considerable sum for Lela's education at the most exclusive Young Ladies' Seminary in the whole of Europe.

Lela had wept when she left her mother.

"If only we were going together Mama," she said, "it would be exciting to see the pictures in the Galleries which you have told me about so often."

"I know, my dearest," her mother answered, "but your Stepfather has been so generous in paying the fees of your School, that I really cannot ask him for anything more at the moment."

Lela had understood because she was well aware that Sir Robert doted on her mother.

He grudged every hour she spent away from him.

Even if they went shopping together he was sometimes disagreeable when they returned, if they had been longer than he had expected.

Lela was sensible enough to be aware that although he did not say anything, he often resented the fact that she was with them when he wanted to be alone with his wife.

She tried to be tactful because she loved her mother, but it was often difficult.

She also knew that it was only when they were alone and could speak without being overheard that her mother would talk to her of her father.

It was then Lela knew that her mother was still miserably unhappy at having lost the only man who had really mattered to her in life.

When she took out his medal to touch it gently, there was an expression on her mother's face which told Lela

33

watching her that nobody could ever take her father's place.

Her mother was longing, although of course she did not say so, to die so that she would be with him again.

This thought came into Lela's mind when she was leaving for Florence, and she clung to her mother saying:

"Promise me, darling Mama, that I can come back for the holidays next year. It will be ghastly being away from you for so long."

"I know, my precious," her mother answered, "and I will try to persuade Sir Robert to bring me on a visit to Florence, although he does not care for the Italians."

'Try, Mama! Please try!" Lela begged.

She made up her mind to learn everything she could because she wanted to please her and the following year Sir Robert and Lady Lawson came to Florence for one weekend.

They were on their way to Rome where Sir Robert wanted to meet some business associates.

Although he was kind and gave Lela a number of presents, she was sure he resented the delight with which mother and daughter greeted each other.

"When can I come home, Mama?" Lela had asked before her Mother said good-bye.

"At the end of the summer term next year," she said. "You will be nearly seventeen, and I want you to help me plan your coming out, which your Stepfather has already promised will be a very brilliant one."

"You mean . . he is giving a Ball for me, Mama?"

"Two, darling, one in London and one in the country."

Her mother held her close for a moment before she said:

"We will buy you some very beautiful clothes, and I am praying that you will find someone as wonderful as your father, who will love you as he loved me."

34

There was a little sob in her voice. Then she added quickly:

"You must work hard this year, for I want you to be not only the most beautiful but also the cleverest debutante."

Lela had laughed, but she was no less determined to try.

As her mother drove away from the School she had a terrifying feeling that she was losing her.

It was a premonition that was sadly proved right.

At the end of the year her mother died unexpectedly having contracted tuberculosis.

Lela could hardly believe it had happened.

Her mother had made no mention in her letters that she was ill, only that at times she was very tired.

Now Lela asked herself bitterly why she had not begged to come home so that she could be with her mother, and why her Stepfather had not sent for her.

His letters, which were few, told her very little, except that she was to stay where she was.

When the time came when she should return home as originally planned, she was told that she was in mourning.

She must remain in Florence until she need no longer wear black.

This meant that she was an exile from England, and had nowhere to go after she had finished her schooling.

Then when she was thinking that she must beg her Stepfather to take her away because it was embarrassing to be so much older than the other girls, an Italian Comtessa sent for her.

She had met her mother on a number of occasions when she was in England, and she now invited Lela to come and live with her.

"What I suggest, my dear," she said, "is that you stay with me in my Villa, which is very comfortable, and keep on with your studies and especially your painting."

35

"I love painting!" Lela exclaimed, "and I copy the pictures in the Uffizi Gallery."

"I know of an excellent teacher who will make you even more proficient than you are already," the *Comtessa* said.

It seemed the solution to all her problems.

There was nothing to draw her back to England now that her mother was dead. Lela wrote to her Stepfather and told him what had been suggested.

Sir Robert had written by return, giving his approval, and sent Lela a large cheque to pay for her further tuition.

Because the *Comtessa* refused to accept anything for staying with her as a guest, Lela felt for the moment she was rich.

She therefore bought the best canvasses and the best paints, and also, on the *Comtessa*'s suggestion, a number of pretty gowns.

"There is no need for you to wear black for any length of time while you are in Italy," the *Comtessa* said.

Because her father and mother had always disliked heavy mourning such as the example set by Queen Victoria, her gowns were mostly mauve and white.

Then after nine months she blossomed into pale pastel colours which made her look even lovelier than she was already.

She was happy and even thinking it would be a mistake to return to England when the *Comtessa* died.

She was in fact very old and fell asleep gently and quietly with a smile on her lips.

It would have been impossible for Lela to mourn her excessively.

After the funeral the *Comtessa*'s family arrived to take possession of the house and its contents.

Lela knew that she must now go back to England.

Her Headmistress made arrangements for her to be

chaperoned by a Diplomat's wife who was returning to England.

She also saw that she was accompanied by a Courier.

Nevertheless she felt very strange when, after having been so long away, she first set foot on English soil.

But she was delighted when she returned to Sir Robert's house in Oxfordshire to find that her old Nurse who had become her mother's lady's maid was still there.

Lela flung her arms around her saying as she did so:

"Nanny, Nanny! I was so afraid you might have left!"

"I was waiting for you, Miss Lela," Nanny said. "Now come upstairs and change after that long and, I am sure, dirty journey."

She spoke in a voice which Lela remembered as a child.

She gave a little choked laugh as she obeyed what she knew was actually an order.

Only when she was in her bedroom, which was the one she had used before she had gone away to School, did she feel instinctively that something was wrong.

"What is it, Nanny?" she asked.

For a moment she thought Nanny was not going to tell her. Then she said:

"I think, Miss Lela, you'll find there's been a few changes at The Towers, and not for the better!"

It was difficult to make Nanny say much, but Lela was soon to discover that the real change was in Sir Robert.

For a start he seemed to have grown very much older and fatter.

There was something different about him that had not been there when her mother had been alive.

It did not take Lela long to realise that, for one thing, he drank very much more than he had in the past.

Besides that, his friends, who seemed always to be in the house, were very different from those he and her mother had entertained.

37

In fact Lela knew her mother would not have approved of them.

Sir Robert had always been a hard rider, and his friends seemed to be the same: hard riding, hard drinking and hard swearing.

They used language in their conversation which shocked Lela, and if anything went wrong they swore as they would have in the hunting-field.

At first they treated her with respect.

Then after only a few days she realised from the 'swimmy' look in their eyes and the way their hands reached out to touch her, that their feelings were something very different.

After Lela's arrival Sir Robert gave a large dinner-party.

One look at the women told Lela that her mother would never have had them in the house.

She had met a great number of the mothers of the girls with whom she had been at School.

She knew that they too would not have invited these women into their homes.

As dinner progressed the laughter grew louder, the women became somewhat abandoned and the men's voices grew thicker.

Lela had never encountered anything like it before.

She was both shocked and disgusted until when the ladies, some of them unsteadily, left the room, she escaped to her bedroom.

She was not surprised to find Nanny waiting there for her.

There was no need for words. She walked into her arms and Nanny held her against her.

"I knew it'd upset you, Dearie," Nanny said, "but the question is what can you do about it?"

It was a question that was to echo and re-echo in Lela's ears all night.

The next morning, after she had been riding, her Stepfather called her into his Study.

She went rather nervously, wondering why he wanted her, and when she had shut the door he said:

"I realise my friends were not good enough for you last night!"

He spoke truculently, and Lela thought how unpleasant he looked and how different from when her mother had been alive.

"I was . . tired," she said after a moment, realising he was waiting for her answer.

"That is a lie!" he replied. "I suppose you were shocked. Well, they are my friends, and now your mother has left me alone. I have to have somebody to keep me company."

"Yes . . of course . . I understand," Lela said softly. "At the same time . ."

"All right! All right!" Sir Robert exclaimed. "But I have a solution to your problem."

Lela looked at him enquiringly, and he said:

"John Hopthorne is coming to see you this afternoon."

Lela tried to remember which of her Stepfather's guests was John Hopthorne.

Then she recalled that she had met him the day after she had arrived, when he had come to luncheon.

He was not a very prepossessing man, but he had been talking to Sir Robert about horses.

She had listened to the conversation because it had interested her.

Now as she thought about it, she remembered Mr. Hopthorne as being a guest last night also.

He had spoken to her before dinner was announced.

She had however been so surprised by the appearance of the ladies as they arrived, that she could not remember one word of what Mr. Hopthorne had said to her.

"What does he want to see me about?" she asked.

"I should have thought that was obvious," Sir Robert replied. "You are a very pretty girl, as more than one man told me last night!"

Lela stared at him.

"Are you . . are you . . saying?" she stammered, thinking her Stepfather could not mean what she thought he meant.

"Hopthorne wants to marry you," Sir Robert said bluntly, "and I have given my consent."

"M . . marry me?" Lela exclaimed. "But . . I could not possibly . . marry him!"

"Why not?"

"He is . . too old . . and I do not . . I . . love him!"

Sir Robert laughed.

"He is very rich, respected in the County, and has his own Pack of Foxhounds. I do not know what more you could want."

"I want a great deal more than that," Lela said quietly, "and my answer is quite simple. It is 'No'!"

Sir Robert looked at her for a moment. Then he said:

"It is unfortunate that you should feel that way about it, as I have already given my consent. I am your Guardian, Lela, and as I have to find a husband for you, I doubt if you could do better than Hopthorne."

He paused, and as Lela said nothing, he went on:

"I have been told on good authority that he will be knighted, either this year or next, for the considerable contribution he has made to the Conservative Party funds."

He laughed, but it was a sound without much humour.

"You will be a Lady, my dear, like I made your mother. There is not a woman born who does not enjoy having a title."

"Then I must be the exception," Lela replied, "for I do not want a title! And I do not wish to be married, at any rate . . not to Mr. Hopthorne!"

There was a moment's silence while Sir Robert scowled at her. Then he said:

"You will do as you are told, and the sooner you are married, the better. I do not want you looking down your nose at my friends, as you did last night, and sneaking away as if they were not good enough for you!"

He suddenly lost his temper and shouted:

"How dare you criticise me! I have looked after you all these years, dressed you, fed you, educated you to please your mother, and now you will do what I say. You will marry Hopthorne, if I have to drag you to the altar!"

Because he sounded so frightening, Lela gave a cry of sheer horror, and turning, ran from the room.

She heard Sir Robert shouting her name as she ran down the passage.

Then she went up the stairs and bursting into her bedroom locked the door.

She threw herself down on the bed, not crying, but trembling and trying desperately to think how she could save herself.

Never in her wildest dreams had she imagined that anything like this could happen when she came back to England.

She was intelligent enough to know that a Guardian had complete control over his Ward.

In her case Sir Robert, as her Stepfather, was her natural Guardian.

Even the Law could not protect her from any decision he might make about her future.

"I will run away!" she told herself.

Just then there was a knock on the door, and she stiffened.

Then she heard Nanny's voice saying:

"It's only me, Miss Lela."

Lela jumped up and let her in.

Then as she looked at Nanny's familiar, loving face, she burst into tears.

"It's all right, it's all right!" Nanny said with her arms around her. "I know what's happened, because Sir Robert told his valet, who told me, that this Mr. Hopthorne wants to marry you."

"But . . I cannot marry him, Nanny . . I cannot marry a man who is so old . . or who could behave as the men were . . behaving last night."

"I know it's something your mother, God rest her, would never want for you, Miss Lela," Nanny said in a low voice, "but what can you do?"

Lela moved herself from Nanny's arms and walked across the room.

She stood looking out at the well-kept garden and the green fields beyond it which was so different from the views she had known in Italy.

Then she said:

"I must run away, Nanny! I shall go back to Italy! We will have somewhere and I will make some money from my painting."

Nanny shook her head.

"I doubt if Sir Robert will let you get away as easily as that, and he'll fetch you home again."

Lela drew in her breath.

Of course Nanny was right and her Stepfather, who was obviously impressed by Mr. Hopthorne, would be determined to assert his authority over her and bring her back to be married.

"Then where can I go? Where can I go?" she asked desperately.

There seemed to be no answer, and she started to pray for her mother.

"Help me, Mama . . help me! You know I cannot . . marry anyone, unless I . . love them in the . . same way

that you . . loved Papa. Help me to escape . . and at least
have a time to think what I . . can do in the . . future."

Then, almost as if her mother was near her, as she
believed she was, she knew the answer.

It came into her mind almost like a flash of lightning.

She turned from the window and said to Nanny:

"I know where I can go where I am sure Step-Papa will
not find me!"

"Where's that, Miss Lela?" Nanny enquired, instinctively looking over her shoulder as if she was afraid somebody might be listening.

"Do you remember Mama's sister?" Lela asked. "I
have had a card from her every Christmas, and she wrote
me a very loving letter when Mama died."

Nanny gave an exclamation.

"Do you mean the Baroness?"

"Yes, of course, Mama's older sister. Although Mama
had not seen her for many years, as she was always
abroad, they regularly wrote to one another."

"Well, now, it's certainly an idea," Nanny agreed, "but
I'm sure Sir Robert will not approve of it."

"Sir Robert is not going to know!" Lela said sharply.

"If he suspects I am running away, he will stop me. I
may even be locked in my room. We have to get away,
Nanny, to escape!"

"Are you expecting me to come with you?" Nanny
asked.

"You know you have to do that," Lela replied. "I
cannot travel alone. I shall need you to look after me."

It was like the cry of a child, and Nanny said:

"I've looked after you ever since you were born, and
no one shall prevent me from doing so now! But are you
sure, dearie, that running away is the only solution?"

"It is the only thing I can do!" Lela replied. "I remember, when Mama wanted to do something, how difficult

it could be once Sir Robert made up his mind to do anything different."

She looked at Nanny pathetically.

"If you had heard him raging at me just now, you would have known that he is absolutely . . determined that I shall . . marry Mr. Hopthorne, whatever I have to . . say on the . . subject."

She felt herself shiver as she spoke, and as if she knew she must convince Nanny she went across to her saying

"Please . . Nanny . . help me . . and although I think . . at the moment that I hate all men . . I want to . . marry some day . . but it must be to . . somebody like Papa."

"Your father was a real Gentleman!" Nanny said.

"Which Sir Robert is not!"

It was something Lela had not thought of before.

She knew that it was what she must have vaguely been aware of from the moment her mother married him.

It was because her mother's friends had loved her that they had accepted Sir Robert's hospitality, both in the country and in London.

Sir Robert, she told herself, was what her father would have called an 'outsider', and Mr. Hopthorne, if he was his friend, was the same.

Lela knew she must be practical and she said to Nanny:

"Pack everything we need, but let no one know what you are doing."

She thought Nanny was indecisive and said:

"It would be a mistake for us to go away empty-handed . . but I would do . . that rather than be kept a . . prisoner here until I . . am a . . bride, and of course it may . . mean that I shall have to . . escape alone."

She knew by the expression on Nanny's face that she would not allow her to do such a thing.

"I'll do as you tells me, Miss Lela," she said, "But you

know how nosey servants can be, and if they've got the slightest idea what we're up to, they'll tell the Master."

"Then it is up to us to be cleverer than they are," Lela said.

She sat talking to Nanny for about an hour, then went downstairs for luncheon.

She found her Stepfather alone in his Study drinking a glass of champagne.

The way he looked up when Lela entered told her that he was slightly ashamed of his behaviour earlier.

She walked across the room to him and said:

"I am sorry if I made you angry, Step-Papa, but what you said took me by surprise."

Her apology made Sir Robert feel even more embarrassed than ever and he said abruptly:

"Forget about it! Would you like a drink?"

"No, thank you," Lela replied, "But I admit to being rather hungry."

"Why the devil is luncheon not ready?" he asked.

He walked to the fireplace and reached out his hand to the bellpull, but at that moment the door opened.

"Luncheon is served, Sir Robert!" the Butler announced.

"And about time too!" Sir Robert said. "Come along, Lela, you said you were hungry!"

Then went into a smaller Dining-room than the one they had used for the party last night.

Lela talked about the horses which Sir Robert had recently bought.

He was determined they would excel those of any other owner in the County.

Only as luncheon finished did he say to Lela:

"You will not forget that Hopthorne is coming to see you this afternoon?"

"No, of course not," Lela answered, "and I was wondering if it would be possible for me to go to London tomorrow or the next day to buy some clothes."

"Clothes?" Sir Robert ejaculated. "That is all women ever think of! But you will undoubtedly want a large number for your trousseau."

He looked at her sharply as he spoke, as if he thought she would protest, but Lela only smiled and said:

"I have only just come home, Step-Papa, and I would like to be with you for a little while."

Her answer obviously took Sir Robert by surprise, then after a moment he answered:

"There is no hurry, take your time, and of course you will need clothes – which inevitably means money!"

He laughed as he spoke as if it was a joke, and Lela smiled.

Then as the carriage was at the door Sir Robert left and she ran upstairs to Nanny.

When John Hopthorne called at four o'clock, Lela wearing one of her prettiest gowns was waiting for him in the Drawing-Room.

When he was announced she looked at him critically, feeling that she was seeing him for the first time.

She knew at once he was a man she could never love in a million years.

There was something about his appearance and the way he walked towards her which told her she was right and he was not the Gentleman that her father had been.

He was an 'Outsider' in the same way that her Step-father was.

"I was hoping to see you alone," John Hopthorne said, "I suppose your Stepfather has told you why I am here?"

He spoke bluntly, but Lela sensed that he was somewhat anxious and unsure of himself.

She did not answer, and after a moment he said:

"Perhaps I had better put it clearly; I am asking you to be my wife!"

46

"Why?" Lela asked.

It was clearly a question John Hopthorne was not expecting, and he answered after a moment:

"You are the prettiest girl I have ever seen!"

Lela waited thinking he must say more. Then after a somewhat uncomfortable silence she said:

"I am of course very honoured by your suggestion, but I think it would be . . wise if we got to . . know each other a . . little better."

"There is no reason for that," John Hopthorne said. "I know that I want you, and I will be wanting you however long we wait."

"But I have met you only twice," Lela said, "and you will understand that as we have not talked together or found out what tastes we have in common, I would like to wait until I know you very much better than I do at the moment."

"I know that I want to marry you," John Hopthorne said in a determined manner, "and I will give you everything you want – within reason."

"I cannot think of anything I want particularly."

John Hopthorne laughed.

"That is something you will not be saying in the future! You will want jewellery, furs, horses and carriages, and I will be very surprised if you do not want to redecorate certain rooms in my house."

"I have not really thought about any of those things," Lela said.

"Well, of one thing you can be certain," John Hopthorne said, "once you are married to me, you will not run short of a penny, and unless you want the moon, I will buy it for you!"

Lela laughed.

"I can see you are very kind," she said, "but I still want time to think about your proposal, and also to get to know you as a man."

"That is more like it!" John Hopthorne said. "And as I want to know you as a woman, I suggest we get a little closer to each other."

He put out his arms as he spoke, but Lela stepped quickly away from him.

Her heart was thumping with fear, but with amazing self-control she appeared calm and unruffled.

"No!" she said.

"Why not?" he asked. "I can tell you that I want to kiss you, which I have wanted to do from the moment I saw you."

"Since I am not . . certain yet that I . . wish to . . kiss you," Lela replied, "that is . . something that . . will have to . . wait."

As if he told himself he should take the initiative, John Hopthorne moved forward to where Lela was standing at the other side of the arm-chair.

"I am going to London tomorrow," she said quickly, "and I will see if there is anything that looks to me like a . . pretty wedding-gown. It is impossible . . to make . . a gown overnight."

John Hopthorne looked at her across the chair.

"What do you say to our being married in three weeks time?" he asked. "That will give the Parson time to publish the Banns."

"I should think making a . . smart wedding-gown will take . . longer than . . that," Lela replied.

"How much longer?"

"I will tell you . . after I have been to . . London!"

"Then I suppose I shall have to be content with that!"

"I could hardly walk up the aisle in a gown that neither fits me nor does justice to my . . Stepfather's . . generosity, or to . . your choice of a bride."

John Hopthorne laughed.

"You are that, all right! Now come along, give me a

kiss to seal the contract, and we will be married in a month."

"No, you are moving too quickly," Lela said.

"And you are playing 'hard to get'," he replied.

"Like any good huntsman you will . . enjoy a good run for your money!". Lela parried.

He laughed again as if he could not help himself.

She still stood behind the chair.

He realised it would seem undignified if he tried to catch her but she managed to escape.

"Very well," he said, "you win for the moment. But make no mistake, Lela, I am a determined chap, and I am always 'in at the kill'!"

Lela wanted to say that was exactly what it would be.

Instead she forced a smile to her lips and said:

"You sound . . rather frightening, and I am . . sure it would be a . . mistake for us . . not to be friends."

"I want to be your husband," John Hopthorne said in a voice that told her he did not understand what she was saying.

"You have made that . . very clear," she answered. "perhaps, as I am going to London . . you could come over later in the week . . and we . . can talk again."

He looked pleased at the suggestion and said after a moment:

"I will do that. Tell your Step-father I will come to dinner on Thursday, and we do not want a large party, just ourselves."

He paused before he added:

"There will be a full moon that night, if you are feeling romantic."

"That is something," Lela replied, "I shall not know until the day after tomorrow."

John Hopthorne looked at her and she thought there was an expression in his face which frightened her.

Then he said.

"I will tell you one thing before I go, you are a damned pretty woman, and I would be proud to have you as my wife!"

He spoke with such effort that Lela had the idea that she ought to applaud him.

Instead she said in a quiet, and what she hoped was a shy voice:

"It is . . very nice . . of you . . to say so."

John Hopthorne turned away as if to go to the door, and Lela came from behind the chair to follow him.

Unexpectedly he turned and caught her in his arms.

"Now I have got you!" he said, "and I will make sure you do not play too many tricks on me!"

He pulled her against him, and knowing he was going to kiss her, she struggled frantically.

He was very strong and she could not break free.

"I want you!" he said. "God, how I want you!"

His voice was hoarse and passionate, and then, because she had turned her face away, he was kissing her cheek and her ear.

She felt revolted by the greedy insistence of his mouth.

"Let me . . go!" she gasped.

"You are mine, and you cannot escape!" he thundered.

She fought desperately to prevent him capturing her lips.

Then when it was almost impossible to breathe and she knew she was weakening, the door opened.

Newman the butler asked in a quiet, respectful voice:

"Would you be requiring tea, Miss Lela?"

Mr. Hopthorne's arms instinctively slackened and Lela fought herself free.

She ran past Newman, out of the Drawing Room, across the hall and up the stairs into her own bedroom.

She slammed the door, then stood with her back against it gasping for breath.

Her heart was beating in an agitated fashion and her lips felt dry.

Nanny was on her knees, packing her trunk.

"What's the matter, dearie? Who's upset you?"

"Quickly . . Nanny!" Lela replied in a voice that did not sound like her own. "We . . have . . to get . . away . . we have to!"

As she spoke she knew if she was forced to marry Mr. Hopthorne, she would kill herself.

Chapter Three

Lela and Nanny left the house at half-past five the following morning.

Lela knew that Sir Robert would be in a deep sleep after drinking too much wine the night before.

He had, as it happened, been far more pleasant when they had dinner alone than he had been the previous evening.

Although, after her encounter with Mr. Hopthorne, she wanted to stay in her room and see no one, she knew it would be a mistake.

If she was to escape from this ghastly trap that was closing around her, she had to be clever.

"Help me . . Papa . ." she prayed.

She felt that only he would understand the danger of her position.

She had therefore talked seemingly quite naturally to Sir Robert about buying new clothes.

"I am afraid, Step-Papa, it will cost you a great deal of money!"

Sir Robert had laughed.

"I do not suppose you will bankrupt me, and of course, having worn mourning for so long, you will want pretty things in pretty colours."

Lela did not say she had been wearing "pretty colours" for the last three months, but merely replied:

"I am sure I shall . . find plenty of . . lovely gowns in London . . but . . how do I . . pay for them?"

She spoke hesitatingly, as if she was embarrassed at asking him for money.

"Put them down to my account," Sir Robert said. "That is something I have at all the best shops."

"I expect there will be . . other things as well," Lela said, "like . . shoes . . gloves and . . hats."

Sir Robert laughed again.

"I suppose you are asking me for some cash! Very well, I will give you £50, but mind you, I shall want an account of it!"

"Of course," Lela agreed, "and thank you very much Step-Papa."

He drank a lot during the dinner and afterwards.

By the time she left him, he had drunk half-a-bottle of port and was beginning to slur his words.

She had however got the money she wanted before she went to bed.

Nanny in the meantime had not been idle, and had borrowed from Newman a Bradshaw's Guide.

This gave the times of the trains, and also, Lela saw with delight, the Schedule of the Steam Navigation Company.

She found that a ship left London from Brunswick Wharf, Blackwell every Wednesday for Rotterdam.

They also sailed on Fridays.

But she thought it was a good omen that they would be able to get away tomorrow, long before Sir Robert had the least suspicion that she would not return.

She had already planned in her mind what she would say in her letter to him.

While Nanny put the gown she had been wearing into her trunk, she sat down at the small *secretaire* in her bedroom and wrote:

Dear Step-Papa,

Thank you very much indeed for the £50, for which I am very grateful. I will try not to be extravagant, but of course, as I do not know London, it may take time to get all the things I require.

I have just remembered that a friend of Mama's wrote to me only a month ago saying that when I returned to England, she would be very pleased if I would stay with her and her family at their house in Mayfair, and also visit them in the country.

I think therefore that Nanny and I might go there for three nights, and perhaps stay with them at their country house for the week-end.

Thank you again for all your kindness,
You affectionate Step-daughter,
Lela.

When she and Nanny left at five-thirty, there were only two footmen to see them off. She gave one of them her letter.

"Give this to Sir Robert when he wakes," she said, "and if he asks why we left so early, say that I thought as we had so much to do the sooner we got to London the better."

"I'll see that th'Master gets your message, Miss," the footman said.

It did not take them long to reach London.

They hired a carriage to Blackwell, rather than waste time trying to find a train from another station.

They caught the Steamer with fifteen minutes to spare, and once they were aboard, Lela gave a sigh of relief.

Nanny however was far more practical than she was.

She tipped a steward to find them good seats, and ordered tea and biscuits.

They were in need of food after travelling for so many hours.

54

As the Steamer moved away from the dock Lela began to feel a sense of adventure and daring which she was sure her father would have understood.

She remembered he once said to her:

"Never be afraid to grasp an opportunity when it presents itself. It is hesitation and indecision which are dangerous in life."

She knew he was thinking of tactics on the battlefield.

She thought it very appropriate at this moment also, as she was fighting a battle against superior odds.

If she was not to be forced into this horrible and frightening marriage, then the only thing she could do was to use tactics which would surprise the enemy.

"How can I marry a man I have seen only twice in my life and for whom I feel an actual revulsion?" she asked.

She remembered the hoarse passion in his voice and what scared her in his eyes.

She had scrubbed her neck until the skin was almost raw because she wanted to forget the feeling of his lips.

She was so intent on her thoughts that she did not notice when they were out at sea that it was somewhat turbulent and many of the passengers were sick.

Nanny survived by having endless cups of strong tea which the steward brought her with a grin.

"Being in the summer this be mild to what we often 'as to put up with," he said.

"Then the sooner you get bigger ships the better!" Nanny, who always managed to have the last word, retorted.

When they reached Rotterdam, it was easy to take a train for The Hague.

Nevertheless, they did not arrive until late in the evening, and Lela was afraid her Aunt might be away.

It was difficult since she had not seen her for years to remember what her Aunt Edith had looked like.

She was sure she would resemble her mother.

From the kind things she had said in the letter she had written after she learned of her death, Lela was quite sure she would be welcome.

An elderly maid opened the door of an attractive red brick house with white surrounds to the window and square gables on the roof.

"Will you please tell *Barones* van Alnradt that her niece is here!" Lela said.

The elderly maid looked at her in astonishment, then at Nanny and the luggage which the cabman was lifting down from their carriage.

"The *Barones* is in bed," she answered, speaking excellent English.

"I am sorry to be so late . ." Lela began.

"She's ill," the maid said, "and has been for some time."

Lela gave a little cry.

"Then I must see her at once! I had no idea she was unwell."

The maid took her up a wooden staircase and opened a door on the First Floor.

"Your niece to see you Madam!" she said abruptly.

Lela entered the room and saw sitting up in bed a very much older replica of her mother.

She saw at first glance that her Aunt was ill, her hair was white and there were deep lines on her face.

At the same time the resemblance was obvious, and she ran eagerly to the bedside to say:

"Aunt Edith, it is Lela! I have come to you because I need your help."

"What a surprise, my dear child!" the *Barones* exclaimed. "And how pretty you are, and exactly like your mother!"

"And you are like her too," Lela replied. "I was afraid I would not remember you, but now I do, and please forgive me for coming here without letting you know."

56

"You are not alone?" the *Barones* asked.

"No, of course not. Nanny is with me, as she has been ever since I was a baby, and she remembers when you came to our house in the country, many years ago."

"I remember it well," the *Barones* said. "But why, dear child, do you need my help?"

"I want to tell you all about it," Lela said, "but please, would it be all right for us to stay here with you? We have nowhere else to go."

"Of course you can stay," the *Barones* replied, "but I cannot understand what has happened. I thought after your mother's death you would be with your Stepfather."

"That is what I am going to explain," Lela said.

The *Barones* rang a bell by her bedside.

"First," she said, "I am sure you will want to take off your travelling things, and have something to eat. Geetruida will look after you and show you where you can sleep."

Lela found that Geetruida was not the only servant in the house, in fact there were three of them, and her Aunt lived comfortably.

The food was excellent if slightly heavy, as Dutch food usually was.

But she had a very pretty bedroom and Nanny was well looked after.

When she told her Aunt what had happened after her mother's death she was horrified.

"But of course you cannot marry a man you have only seen twice," she exclaimed, "and who is so much older than you! It is disgraceful of Sir Robert to suggest such a thing, and I shall tell him so if I see him!"

Lela gave a cry of horror.

"But you must not see him, and neither must I!" she said. "When Step-Papa has made up his mind about something, even Mama had the greatest difficulty in making him change it. In fact she usually failed."

"Then you will just have to hide yourself here until we think of a solution," the *Barones* said.

"That is what I was hoping you would allow me to do," Lela said, "and it will be lovely to be with you and be able to talk about Mama and Papa."

"I loved your mother very dearly," the *Barones* answered. "We had a great deal in common even though she was ten years younger than I was. But as my late husband was a Diplomat we were continually travelling, and I therefore saw far too little of her after I married."

She held out her hand to Lela.

"But having you here will make up for my missing Mildred, although I am afraid you, dear child, will find it very dull."

"I am sure that is impossible," Lela said. "As I drove through the town from the station, I could see how beautiful The Hague is, and of course I want to visit the famous Museums."

"You have heard of them?" the *Barones* asked in surprise.

"In the Art School in Florence they talked about the pictures in Holland, and I think they were a little jealous of your Rubens and Rembrandts!"

The *Barones* laughed.

"As a country, we have a unique position in the Art World, and of course in Florence they taught you to love and understand paintings."

"I myself have been having special lessons in painting for the last year," Lela said.

"I wish my husband was still alive," the *Barones* said. "When he retired he took up painting. Of course he had always been a collector of art, and he said that at last he had time to be an artist!"

"I do hope you have some of his pictures for me to see," Lela said.

"Quite a number of them," the *Barones* replied, "and what is more, you can use his Studio."

Lela's eyes lit up.

"Are you sure you would not mind my doing that?"

"I would love you to," her Aunt replied, "and you will find everything you need there. But first you must visit the Mauritshuis which, as I expect you already know, is the most famous Museum of painting we have in The Hague."

"Of course I am longing to do that," Lela said.

That night she went to bed early because she was very tired.

The next day on her Aunt's instructions, she went up to the attic and found the most delightful studio she had ever imagined.

The *Baron* had certainly been determined to make the most of his artistic talent.

He had put in a large North window, which every artist requires to give him the best possible conditions for painting.

The ceiling was surprisingly high for an attic and the walls were covered with pictures he had painted, many of them copies of the famous Masters.

Having explored the Studio, Lela ran excitedly downstairs to thank her Aunt for saying she could use it.

She found the *Barones* looking rather pale and with deep lines under her eyes.

"How do you feel, Aunt Edith?" she asked.

"I had a bad night, my dear."

"It is not my fault, I hope?"

"The excitement of your coming here may have had something to do with it," her Aunt admitted, "but I am, I am afraid, a very ill woman."

Lela sat down beside the bed.

"I feel very ashamed I have not asked you about it

before," she said, "but I did not realise you were . . seriously ill."

"I have a growth in my inside," her Aunt said, "and although the Doctors wish to chop me about, I will not allow it."

Her Aunt put out a thin white hand to take hers.

"I think you will understand, my dear," she said, "that I have no wish to live to be very old, in any case major operations are seldom very successful."

"But Aunt Edith . ." Lela began to protest.

Her Aunt silenced her with a gesture of her other hand.

"If you are going to live with me, I think I should explain my position," she said. "I loved my husband very dearly and without him I feel very lonely."

She paused to look at Lela searchingly before she went on:

"Had I been fortunate enough to have a child of my own, things would have been different. I have in fact two Stepsons, but although Johan is very kind to me, he is away at the moment in Java, where he is the Governor of the Province."

Lela was listening intently, aware as she held her Aunt's hand that it was very cold.

"When the Doctors first told me I needed an operation," the *Barones* went on, "they said there was a fifty-fifty chance of it being successful. But they also told me that it would be very expensive."

Lela looked at her in surprise and she said:

"I have enough money on which to live provided I am careful, but not enough for any large expenditure, such as surgery in Holland would cost."

Lela did not know what to say, and her Aunt continued:

"I did however consider writing to my Stepson Johan when his brother Nicolaes began behaving in a very disgraceful manner."

"What did he do?" Lela asked.

"He ran up debts, then tried to persuade me to sell some of the pictures from this house which my husband had left especially to Johan, and when I refused he became very disagreeable."

Her voice sharpened.

"I knew then that if I left the house and went to hospital, he would take the pictures and it would be difficult for anybody to stop him."

"I have never heard of anything so disgraceful!" Lela declared. "But you surely cannot refuse to have an operation if it will cure you?"

"I have no wish to live," the *Barones* said, "and it would be a waste of the money which Johan will need when I am gone, as he has a large family."

"You cannot leave it . ." Lela began, but the *Barones* checked her.

"I have no wish to argue any more about it. I am sometimes in pain, but the Doctors have given me something to prevent it from overwhelming me. However it will make all the difference to have you here, and perhaps I shall feel so happy that by a miracle I shall be cured!"

"I do not like to . . think of you . . suffering," Lela said, "and Nanny told me that Mama felt terribly . . tired before she died."

There was a sob in her voice which she could not prevent, and her Aunt said:

"I am sure, my dear, that your mother is near you now, and is glad that we are together."

"Of course she is!" Lela agreed. "In fact I think it was Mama who sent me to you when I was feeling desperate at the idea of being forced into marriage with Mr. Hopthorne."

"I am certain that is true," the *Barones* agreed. "Now I am tired of talking about myself, and as you are a painter like my husband, I have a commission for you."

"A commission?" Lela exclaimed.

"It is a rather fascinating story," the *Barones* said. "My husband became great friends with Des Tombe who was a well-known collector of pictures."

The *Barones* laughed as she said:

"They used to sit for hours talking over different paintings, and I have never known two men to be more absorbed in any subject!"

"I think all artists become dedicated to their work," Lela smiled.

"That is true, dear, and it was my husband who persuaded Des Tombe to leave Johan Vermeer's *Head of a Girl* to the Mauritshuis when he died."

Lela knew that Vermeer was one of the most important painters in Holland in the seventeenth-century.

She did not interrupt as the *Barones* continued:

"It seems incredible, but Des Tombe acquired the Vermeer portrait for his collection for only two guilders and thirty cents. Now, of course, it has been acclaimed as one of the greatest of his paintings, and it has just been hung in the Mauritshuis."

"Then I shall see it! How exciting!" Lela exclaimed.

"You will not only see it, but I want you also to copy it for me. As you realise, I am too ill to go to the Museum myself."

"But of course I will do that," Lela said, "and it will be very exciting for me!"

"It will make me very happy," her Aunt smiled. "I have heard so much about this wonderful portrait that I almost feel as if the girl it depicts is one of the family!"

They both laughed, and Lela said:

"I will go to the Mauritshuis this afternoon, and I suppose I may take one of the canvasses that are upstairs in the Studio?"

"Of course you may, dear, but at the same time be careful to choose one of the right period."

Lela looked puzzled and her Aunt explained.

"My husband was a perfectionist, and when he started to paint he was determined to use canvasses of the century of whatever picture he was copying, so he collected them wherever he could."

"What a clever idea!" Lela exclaimed.

"That is what I thought," her Aunt replied, "and you will find them all upstairs, together with the right paints. They are all neatly labelled because my husband was very meticulous about such things."

"Thank you for giving me something so exciting to do!" Lela said. "I only hope I shall do justice to Vermeer's beautiful girl."

She set off immediately after luncheon with Nanny for the Museum.

She had found a canvas exactly as her Aunt had described, which was of the seventeenth-century.

There was in fact a stack of them in one corner of the Studio.

She saw that some of them were painted on already, but with rather bad pictures which she supposed the *Baron* intended to erase.

She could understand that in his desire for perfection the canvas would be very important.

Similarly the paints, which were also labelled, were arranged on shelves.

There was no possibility of her using paints of the wrong constituents.

The Mauritshuis Museum was, as she had expected, in a very attractive house which had been the private residence of one of the most important men in Dutch history.

Last night, before she was too tired to talk any more, Lela had persuaded her Aunt to tell her about Johan Maurits Van Nassau who was the founder of the Museum.

"He was one of my husband's heroes," the *Barones* said, "and like the people in the pictures he copied. I cannot help thinking that Johan Maurits is a close friend from whom I can never escape!"

Lela laughed.

Her Aunt had gone on to explain how Johan Maurits had fought the Spaniards in Brazil, besides having an absorbing interest in everything that was new and unusual.

Then she added:

"In fact, he was a combination of the old world and the new, the physical and the spiritual, which is very rare in men all over the world."

As Lela thought of him and looked at his portrait, she could not help thinking that was the sort of man she would like to marry.

He would be both brave and adventurous!

At the same time he would be consciously aware of the things which belonged to the "World beyond the World" in which he was living.

"I do not suppose men like that exist today," she thought a little sadly.

She then began to feel excited at the picture she was to copy for her Aunt.

When she had sat in the Uffizi Gallery in Florence copying a painting by Botticelli, her teacher had been pleased with her efforts.

He had said when she started:

"You have to 'feel' what you are painting, and although you are copying a great Master, I want to find something of yourself in the picture when it is finished."

Lela had understood what he was trying to tell her.

When at the end of the year he praised her work, she had known that she was in fact his best pupil, and he was proud of her.

Now she was determined that she would make her Aunt happy.

Perhaps to have Vermeer's *Head of a Girl* on her bedroom wall would make her forget for a time the pain she suffered.

"She ought to have the operation, Nanny!" she had said after relating what her Aunt had told her.

"That's what they're all saying in the house," Nanny answered. "But it's something she can't afford, and I understand all the pictures and furniture have been left to the new *Baron*, who is in Java."

"Yes, that is right, that is what Aunt Edith said," Lela replied. "But I am sure if he knew how ill she looks he would want her to try anything to get better."

"Then you must see what you can do to help her," Nanny said, "and they're saying in the kitchen that having you here is the best thing that could have happened!"

When they reached the Mauritshuis, Lela had no difficulty in finding the Vermeer masterpiece.

As she passed through the rooms she wanted to stop and stare at the other pictures.

But she had the feeling it was urgent that she should start work on her Aunt's picture, so she hurried on to where it was hanging.

It was certainly very lovely.

As she stared at it she could understand in a way why the *Baron* had been so obsessed by it.

There was something unusual in the painting of the girl looking over her shoulder with her mouth slightly open, an expression in her eyes as if she was curious.

Lela could understand too that the portrait had depth and colour.

Also that indescribable sense of reality which could only come from an artist of genius.

At the same time, the painting was not really difficult to copy as a more complicated scene might have been.

The blue and yellow scarf around the girl's head, the one translucent pearl in her ear, and her plain green and yellow gown were merely a matter of getting the paints right, and following in the Master's path.

Nanny was carrying the small easel and a folding stool which had been used by the *Baron*.

As soon as they were set in place Lela picked up her palette and started to work.

She had brought her own paintbox with her in her luggage, but now she was using the *Baron*'s.

The paints that he had labelled as being right for the seventeenth-century.

Nanny seated herself near a window.

Bringing out her crochet, she started to work on a long strip of lace which was intended for a sheet.

Lela thought it would be a nice present for her Aunt, as she was always confined to her bed.

She worked for over two hours until Nanny said it was time to go home.

"I cannot leave now!" Lela protested, but Nanny insisted.

"There's no sense in doing too much too quickly!" she said, "and I knows your Aunt'll be looking forward to seeing you."

That was undoubtedly true, and Lela therefore let herself be taken back.

She was excited by what she had done already.

She had worked in exactly the way her teacher would have wanted her to.

When they arrived at the house Lela refused to show her Aunt what she had done so far, saying that it was to be a surprise when it was finished.

She talked to her instead of what she and her mother had done in the old days, until her Aunt's eyes closed and she fell asleep.

Lela went quickly away and downstairs to where she found a great number of books that she wanted to read.

There were also some pictures that she knew were not

66

only beautiful, but valuable, and were part of the *Baron*'s collection.

She had already learned from her Aunt how he had saved up every penny he could to buy pictures in all the countries to which they travelled.

She thought it would be a great pity for his collection to be broken up by his son Nicolaes.

It must certainly be kept intact for the elder brother.

The next morning Lela was back at the Mauritshuis working until luncheon-time, and then went back again in the afternoon.

She was concentrating on her work when suddenly became aware that somebody was standing just behind her.

She thought at first it was one of the sightseers in the Museum who often looked over her shoulder, no doubt thinking they could do better themselves.

Then a voice said:

"I think you are Jungfrau Lela Cavendish, who is staying with *Barones* van Alnradt!"

Lela turned to look up at the man who had spoken, and saw he was short and thin with a grey beard.

"Yes, I am," she admitted.

"Then I am delighted to meet you," he said, "I am Jan Nijsted and I knew the *Baron* very well."

Lela smiled and he went on:

"In fact, I am a picture-dealer and sold some of the pictures he painted; not those he copied, but his original creations."

"How interesting!" Lela said.

At the same time she was wishing the stranger would go away and allow her to get on with her painting.

"I see you are very experienced, Miss Cavendish," Mr. Nijsted said. His English was excellent.

"I would like to think so," Lela answered. "I have been

studying in Florence, and I am making this copy for my Aunt."

"You know that your Aunt is ill?" Mr. Nijsted said, "and that she should have an operation if she is to live?"

Lela looked at him in surprise.

She had no idea her Aunt's condition was common knowledge.

Then she remembered that if he was a close friend, he would obviously know that her Aunt was confined to her bed.

Mr Nijsted lowered his voice, although there was nobody near enough to overhear them.

"I also know that your Aunt cannot afford the services of the best Surgeon in Amsterdam, and that, Miss Cavendish, is why I have a proposition to put to you."

Lela looked at him in surprise and he went on:

"As I was such a close friend of the *Baron* for many years I know he would not want his son Nicolaes, who is a ne'er-do-well, to sell the pictures he collected so painstakingly."

"No, of course not," Lela agreed, "and I was wondering in fact if I ought to write to my Aunt's other Stepson Johan to tell him what is happening."

"As it would take a long time for a letter to reach him in Java, and even longer for his reply to get here," Mr. Nijsted said, "I have something different to suggest to you."

Lela wondered what he could be talking about and she reluctantly put down her palette and paintbrushes and listened.

"There is a nobleman over here from England," Mr. Nijsted said, "who is anxious to acquire some of the very best Dutch pictures."

It flashed through Lela's mind that he was going to suggest that she gave him one of the *Baron*'s pictures to sell and she stiffened.

Then he said:

"I can see from the way you work that you are exceptionally proficient, and you are also using the right canvas and the right paints. I would therefore like to offer the copy you are making to this Englishman."

Lela stared at him in absolute astonishment.

"You cannot be . . suggesting. . ." she stammered, looking up from her canvas to the head of the girl which was hanging on the wall just above her.

"What I am suggesting, Miss Cavendish," Mr. Nijsted replied, "is that your portrait, with its seventeenth-century paints and canvas is the rough sketch done by Vermeer for the portrait we are both looking at at this moment!"

Lela drew in her breath. Then she said indignantly:

"Are you saying we should deliberately lie and deceive him!"

Mr. Nijsted made a very eloquent gesture with his hand.

"What is the alternative, Miss Cavendish? That you let your Aunt die? What you would receive for this painting if the English nobleman accepts it as a sketch for Vermeer's portrait, would pay for the operation and perhaps prolong her life for twenty years."

Lela turned her head away from him.

"It is quite . . impossible!" she said. "I have. . . nothing more to say!"

"I am surprised," Mr. Nijsted said, "that you have so little affection for your Aunt, when I know your arrival has been the best thing that could have happened to her when she was so depressed and lonely."

He paused for a moment before he said:

"I wish you could have seen her when the *Baron* was alive. She was so happy, so lovely and lively and witty, and everybody in The Hague loved her."

Lela was trying not to listen as he went on:

"The *Baron* used to tell me what a success she was in

the foreign countries in which they lived when he was a Diplomat. She was very different then from the sad woman she has become now."

There was silence. Then, as if he forced her to speak Lela said:

"My Aunt would not . . wish me to lie or to . . try and deceive anybody!"

"If you asked her, of course she would say no," Mr. Nijsted said, "and she will die, I believe, very soon. The cancer from which she is suffering grows more rapidly every day the operation does not take place."

Lela wanted to scream at him to go away and not torture her with such words.

Then almost, she thought, as if he was Satan tempting her, Mr. Nijsted said very quietly;

"Surely the end justifies the means when it is a question of taking a little money from a very rich man and saving a very wonderful woman's life?"

"How can I . . possibly do . . such a . . thing?" Lela asked despairingly.

She had the frightening feeling that if Mr. Nijsted went on talking to her, she would find it hard not to agree to his outrageous suggestion.

Chapter Four

The Marquis, thanks to his brilliant organisation, reached his yacht at Greenwich before noon the following morning.

He had made all his arrangements before he did so.

He had written very plausible letters to his friends like Willy, telling them that he had heard of a sale of pictures in Amsterdam which he must attend.

He wrote:

The King pointed out to me recently that I was short of Dutch Masters in my Gallery, and this was certainly a smear on what I intend to be the most comprehensive private Picture Gallery in England.

You will understand therefore that there was nothing else I could do, having heard of this particular sale, but leave for Holland immediately. . .

When he had finished it he read the letter and decided it sounded convincing.

He sent a telegram first thing in the morning to Amsterdam, then crossed the Channel.

He was running away and going into hiding, but it was the only possible thing he could do in the circumstances.

His new yacht the *Heron* made the crossing in what the Marquis was sure was record time, and he entered the Noordzee Kanaal.

This was the widest and deepest canal in the world with the largest locks.

It had been opened in 1876 to save ships from having to sail a long way up the coast to enter the huge harbour of Amsterdam.

The Noordzee Kanaal was fifteen miles long, and had been a triumph of Dutch engineering.

The *Heron* crossed the busy port on the Marquis's orders to the end of the Heerengracht Kanaal.

This was known in English as "The Gentleman's Canal".

On each side of the concentric canal built centuries earlier were the lovely 17th century houses of the Merchant Millionaires, whose ships sailed home from the East down the Zuider Zee.

It was late when they tied up alongside, and the Marquis went straight to bed.

He was having his breakfast in the Saloon next morning when his friend Count Hans Ruydaal came aboard.

He was a good-looking young Dutchman, the same age as the Marquis, and they had been friends for years.

"I was surprised, Carew," the Count said, "to receive your telegram, but delighted you are here!"

They shook hands, and the Count sat down at the table saying:

"Now, what is the reason for this sudden visit? And do not tell me it is because you have been yearning to see me!"

He laughed as he spoke, and the Marquis replied:

"I have come to buy some Dutch Masters for my Picture Gallery. His Majesty actually noticed that I am short of them!"

The Count's eyes twinkled as he answered:

"You will have to give me a better reason than that for this sudden passion for Holland, and I am quite certain it is a question of *Cherchez la femme!*"

The Marquis laughed.

"Stop interrogating me, Hans, and help me to go home with some good pictures to explain my absence."

"We have, as you know," the Count replied, "enough pictures to fill a million galleries, but as you will want only the best, you will have to be careful. Of course, I will put you in touch with Dealers whom you can trust."

"I was sure you would!" the Marquis said complacently.

"But the first thing I want to know," Hans said, "is whether you want to stay with the Queen at The Hague. You know that Her Majesty would be delighted to have you."

"You have not told her of my arrival?" the Marquis asked.

As he spoke he thought with dismay that if Queen Wilhelmina was aware that he was in Holland, he would have to spend his time in the *Huis ten Bosch* or "House in the Wood".

This was where the Royal Family preferred to live, only using the Palace in Amsterdam for official purposes.

"I have not yet told Her Majesty," Count Hans said. "I was waiting until I knew exactly what you wanted to do."

"What I do not want," the Marquis said firmly, "is to spend my time bowing and scraping and meeting an interminable number of serious-minded Dutchmen who will prevent me from enjoying my stay with you."

The Count put back his head and laughed.

"I thought that would be your attitude," he said, "so having received your telegram I have not mentioned your arrival to anyone except my Housekeeper."

"I should much enjoy being with you," the Marquis said. "Alternatively, I could sleep here on the yacht."

"You cannot expect me not to be hospitable," Count Hans said, "but if you wish to be grand and also in

73

Amsterdam, you can of course be accommodated in the *Koninklijk Paleis.*"

This was the Palace in the Dam Square in the centre of the town around which everything revolved.

The Marquis knew the *Paleis* which had been built originally as a Town Hall and looked like a Town Hall.

It was, he thought, so large and pompous that he knew he would dislike every moment he had to spend in it.

He had always thought it showed very good taste on the part of the Royal Family.

Despite the three hundred rooms in the *Paleis*, they had managed to accommodate themselves comfortably in their very pretty Palace in The Hague.

"Very well," the Count was saying, "you can stay with me, but if you are uncomfortable, I refuse to accept any blame for it."

"You are being ultra-modest," the Marquis replied. "I have been to your house, and it is the sort of bachelor establishment which is exactly what I want at the moment."

The Count looked at him quizzically.

"I knew it was a question of *Cherchez la femme*!"

"Two of them!" the Marquis said bitterly. "But I have no wish to talk about it."

"Inevitably you have made me curious," the Count said. "The trouble with you, Carew, is that you are too good-looking, too rich, and too damned successful. There has to be a snag somewhere. If it is a woman who has got under your skin, I am sure it is good for your ego!"

"Leave my ego alone," the Marquis replied, "and let us talk about pictures! I shall have to take some back with me, and if they are not of the very finest quality, and what my friends will consider a "snip", our friendship is at an end!"

The Count only laughed.

When the Marquis finished his breakfast, the two

friends walked along the tree-lined bank of the Kanaal to the Count's very attractive house.

It was furnished with the idea of comfort rather than beauty.

At the same time there were pictures which the Marquis would have been delighted to possess.

Moreover, as in most of the houses on this canal, there was an elegant curved staircase topped by a painted ceiling.

Many of the rooms had exquisitely plastered ceilings, and some of them had fine panelling.

He thought there was nowhere else in the world where he would find so many beautiful old houses in such a picturesque setting.

As in so many of the old buildings there was a large hook on top of the roof.

It was a reminder of the days when the valuable merchandise of spices was hauled to the upper storeys for safety, protected by the merchant's family, who lived on the lower floors.

The two friends enjoyed a glass of excellent wine before they drove in the Count's carriage into the City.

As they travelled through the busy streets he said:

"I am afraid, Carew, that you will not be able to keep your arrival quiet, and, however much you may protest, you will have to call on Her Majesty. After all she was very fond of your father, and stayed at Kyne.

"Of course I will do that," the Marquis said, "and I shall in fact be delighted to see Queen Wilhemina again. At the same time you must make it clear that I am here on business, and must therefore be in Amsterdam, and not at The Hague.

"I will do my best," the Count promised, "and I will also try to provide you with some charming and attractive women who you may find more alluring than anything you see on canvas!"

The Marquis was about to say that the one thing he did not want at the moment was to meet women and that he disliked them all.

Then he knew the strength of his feelings would be too revealing even to an old friend like Hans.

The Marquis made it a rule never to speak about his love-affairs and he despised men who did so.

He therefore simply told himself firmly that, however attractive the women that Hans produced for him, he had no intention of becoming involved with any of them.

He had learned a lesson which would last him for years, if not for his lifetime.

In The Hague Lela was battling with her conscience.

She was trying wildly to find some excuse for not agreeing to what she knew was an outrageous suggestion by Mr. Nijsted.

Before she met the *Barones* that afternoon she had promised she would think over his suggestion and tell him her answer the next morning.

As she walked home Nanny asked her:

"What was that gentleman talking to you about, Miss Lela?"

"He was a friend of the *Baron*," Lela replied.

She did not say any more, and they walked on in silence until Nanny said:

"He had a lot to say for himself! You be careful when you're talking to strange gentlemen who haven't been introduced to you!"

"He knew all about Aunt Edith's illness," Lela answered, "and I am afraid she is worse than I had thought."

"So they tells me," Nanny agreed. "I shouldn't be surprised if she died very quickly before anyone does anything about it."

When Lela was alone in her bedroom that night she asked her mother what she should do.

76

"It is . . wrong and. . . wicked to be so. . . deceitful," she said, "and if it is . . discovered that I have deliberately tricked an Englishman, I might be sent to . . prison!"

She covered her face with her hands and went on:

"Help me . . Mama! Tell me . . what I . . should do! Shall I try to save Aunt Edith by doing . . something which I am . . sure is . . wrong?"

She hardly slept that night, tossing and turning until morning came.

Then she went upstairs to the *Baron*'s Studio to collect another canvas the same size as the one she had taken before.

Nanny was curious as to why she should want it, but she gave her an evasive answer.

When they arrived at the Mauritshuis, Nanny went to her usual seat in the window, and started to crochet.

Lela propped the canvas on which she had been working against the wall and put the new canvas on her easel.

She began again to paint in the head of the girl, as she done had previously.

She had been working for half-an-hour when Mr. Nijsted arrived.

He walked up to her and although she was conscious of him standing behind her, she did not speak.

He looked at the unfinished painting on the floor, and above it Vermeer's original for some minutes before he said:

"It is excellent! I congratulate you, Miss Cavendish, on having a real talent."

"Take the . . picture! Take . . it!" Lela said almost violently. "I do not . . want to think . . about it . . or hear what you have to . . say when you . . sell it. It is . . wrong! I know what we are . . doing is . . wrong . . but if it saves my Aunt from . . dying . . perhaps God will . . forgive me."

"I am sure He will do that," Mr. Nijsted said. "However it is not a question of my taking it to the Marquis of Kyneston, Miss Cavendish, but for you to show it to him!"

Lela put down her palette and paintbrush and stared at Mr. Nijsted incredulously.

"I . . I show it?" she asked after a moment. "Do you expect me . . to . . take it to . . him?"

"Of course," Mr. Nijsted said. "I cannot tell a story which is yours."

"I . . I do not . . understand."

"It is quite simple," he said. "You have come to stay with your Aunt but find her very ill and unable to afford an operation which the Surgeons say is urgent if her life is to be saved."

Lela made a little murmur, but she did not speak and Mr. Nijsted went on:

"You searched the house for something you could sell to pay the cost of the operation, knowing there was no time to consult *Baron* Johan van Alnradt, who is in Java, and who has been left his father's collection."

Mr. Nijsted paused for a moment as if to make the story more dramatic before he continued:

"Then, almost like a miracle, you found in the *Baron*'s Studio this picture which you think – you are almost sure – is a sketch made by Vermeer prior to painting *The Head of a Girl* which now hangs in the Mauritshuis."

Mr. Nijsted lowered his voice as he said:

"You have told no one what you have found because you are afraid if you do so Nicolaes van Alnradt, who is known to be trying to grab any picture he can lay his hands on, may hear of it."

He looked at her to see if she was listening before he went on:

"Instead, as you have been told of the arrival of the Marquis of Kyneston who like yourself is English, you have brought the picture to him, knowing you can trust

78

him, while you might, in your ignorance, easily he cheated by a Dutch Dealer."

When Mr. Nijsted stopped speaking there was a smile almost of triumph on his lips, as if he was delighted with his story.

Listening, Lela was aware of the way his mind worked.

She had to admit that it was a clever tale with just enough truth about it to make it sound completely plausible.

Then instinctively, because she was frightened, she said quickly:

"I . . I cannot do it!"

Mr. Nijsted flung up his hands in a gesture that was more eloquent than words.

He did not reply, and after a moment she asked piteously:

"How . . can I? How can I do . . anything like that? If the Marquis becomes aware of my deception . . I could be denounced as a . . a . . forger!"

"Not if you stick to the story as I have told it," Mr. Nijsted said slowly as if speaking to a child. "You found this sketch in the *Baron*'s Studio, you have no idea who has painted it, but you know that the *Baron* was a close friend of Des Tombe, who gave the Vermeer to the Mauritshuis Gallery."

He was very persuasive as he continued:

"It is easy therefore to imagine he at the same time bought the sketch which Vermeer made for the picture, which is what most artists do before they embark on a major work."

Lela knew this was true and Mr. Nijsted went on:

"Then he must have kept it in his house, not intending to reveal his possession of it until Vermeer's finished masterpiece was hung in the Gallery."

Again Lela thought it was a good explanation, which

might be accepted by anybody who had no reason to be suspicious.

As if he knew what she was thinking, Mr. Nijsted said:

"Who could imagine for a moment that a girl as young as yourself, and who is not known to have any particular artistic ability, could copy Vermeer's work so skilfully, and with the correct paints and canvas of the period in which he lived?"

"I . . . suppose it is a. . . strange coincidence," Lela admitted as if the words were forced from between her lips.

"So strange, in fact, that no one will question such a story for one moment," Mr. Nijsted said. "So, Miss Cavendish, you have to be brave and remember only that you are saving your Aunt's life."

"If I . . do . . deceive the Marquis," Lela said hesitatingly, "h . . how shall I . . tell him what . . money I require and . . how much I should . . ask?"

"That is something in which you will not be involved," Mr. Nijsted said. "When the Marquis asks you what the sketch is worth or what you want for it, you tell him the truth, that you have no idea."

Lela looked at him wide-eyed.

"You will also say that you have not mentioned your find to your Aunt, but you have thought of getting in touch with Jan Nijsted, who both bought and sold pictures for the *Baron*, and was in fact his close friend."

"Surely the Marquis will ask me why I have not already done so?" Lela said sharply.

"If he does," Mr. Nijsted replied, "you look shy and girlish and say that as you know so little about Holland, having only just arrived here, you thought it would be wiser to trust an Englishman rather than a Dutchman, whom you have never met."

"I see you have thought it all out very cleverly," Lela

80

said. "But I am . . frightened . . I am frightened of . . doing something which I know is . . wrong."

"But because you have come here today, bringing the canvas which is nearly completed, and have started on another one, I know," Mr. Nijsted said gently, "that you intend to save your Aunt at the expense of your conscience."

"Very well," Lela said. "But if it is I who . . have to go to the Marquis . . how shall I do so?"

"A carriage will be waiting for you at one o'clock" Mr. Nijsted said, "and I suggest you have an early luncheon, then travel to Amsterdam with the old woman you have brought with you, but on no account are you to tell her what you are doing."

"She will be very curious."

"You can say that I have entrusted you with a parcel to take to the Marquis because he is English, and I have sworn you to secrecy as to its contents."

Lela sighed.

"More lies . . more subterfuge," she thought.

She knew it would be very difficult to deceive Nanny.

"Now just carry out my instructions," Mr. Nijsted said, a note of authority in his voice. "When I bring you the money for your Aunt's operation, you can get in touch with the Doctors and say they can go ahead with the operation. Then you will be sure you have done the right thing."

"I can . . only hope . . so," Lela said miserably.

Without saying any more, Mr. Nijsted went away.

She went on painting, feeling it was hard to concentrate on anything but the ordeal which lay ahead of her.

It was half-past eleven when she suggested to Nanny that they should go home.

"Why so early?" she asked.

"We are going into Amsterdam after luncheon," Lela replied.

"Is it something to do with the gentleman who was talking to you just now?"

"Yes, Nanny, he has asked me to take a parcel to the Marquis of Kyneston, who has apparently just arrived in Amsterdam, and he is lending me his carriage."

"The Marquis of Kyneston?" Nanny asked. "Now why should you have anything to do with him, I'd like to know?"

"Have you heard of him?" Lela asked.

"Quite enough to know he is somebody you should not be associating yourself with unless you are properly chaperoned, as your mother would wish you to be."

"I only have to take him a parcel from Mr. Nijsted."

"I should have thought he's healthy and strong enough to carry his own parcel!" Nanny remarked tartly.

"It is because the Marquis is . . English and I am . . English too!" Lela said.

"Well, it certainly seems strange to me!" Nanny said, "and I'm sure your Aunt would disapprove if she knew you were careering off to meet a man you don't know, just because he's English!"

"Oh, please, Nanny, you must not tell Aunt Edith and upset her," Lela said. "I am sure that like me you will enjoy seeing Amsterdam which I might not otherwise have had the opportunity of doing so, as Aunt Edith is so ill."

"I was talking to her coachman last night," Nanny related, "and she's got a nice carriage, and a horse, which although he's getting old, is still quite strong. I think we might drive around and have a look at the town, when you're not painting as though your life depended on it!"

"I think that is a good idea," Lela answered, "but I have promised now to go to Amsterdam, and of course you will have to come with me."

"I should hope so!" Nanny said. "Your mother

wouldn't want you gallivanting about a City all by your-self! And I'm sure the Marquis'll think it very strange!"

"Then we will leave at one o'clock," Lela said.

Although Nanny grumbled, Lela had the feeling that she wanted to see Amsterdam as much as she did herself.

It would be exciting going there in a comfortable carriage which they found was drawn by two horses.

Lela put on one of the prettiest gowns she had brought from Florence and a hat that seemed almost like a halo on her fair hair.

When she was alone in her bedroom she packed up the canvas very carefully and carried it down the stairs before Nanny joined her.

She hoped it would escape her notice.

But when it was laid opposite to them on the small seat, Nanny said suspiciously:

"That parcel you're taking to the Marquis looks to me the same size as the picture you were painting on the easel."

"Oh, Nanny, you are not to ask questions! I promised Mr. Nijsted I would not discuss with anybody else what he wants the Marquis to see, and I cannot break my word."

Nanny sniffed, and was obviously offended that she was being kept out of something secret.

They drove for at least a mile in silence.

Lela was thrilled with the windmills they were passing, the canals on one side of them, and the trees which took away the austerity of the land that was so flat it seemed to vanish into the distant horizon.

Then at last they were in Amsterdam.

Now there were the beautiful houses that Lela had read about.

Also romantic bridges over the canals which made her aware that the whole City was built on water.

She could see the tall spires of the Churches as they drove through the narrow, crowded streets.

She thought how excited she would be if it was not for the hard lump of fear in her breast.

She was sure that Mr. Nijsted would have arranged a time for her to meet the Marquis.

When the coachman turned his horses down the very narrow street running parallel with a canal she felt her fear increase until it was hard to breathe.

Each house seemed to her to be more picturesque and more spectacular than the last.

They drew up outside one that was particularly outstanding.

Now she could only think that in a few minutes she would have to lie and lie convincingly.

As she bent forward to pick up the canvas she knew her hands were trembling.

The footman got down from the box and rang the bell.

When the door was opened he assisted Lela from the carriage.

Nanny followed her and they walked up the steps and into what she saw was a very beautiful panelled hall with a curving staircase rising to the floor above.

Lela and Nanny stood for a moment until a servant wearing what seemed to be rather a strange livery said:

"If you are Jungfrau Cavendish, His Lordship is waiting to receive you."

"I'll wait here," Nanny said.

She seated herself on a wooden chair which bore the Count's coat-of-arms.

Feeling very small and frightened, Lela followed the servant.

He flung open the door of a room where the sunshine was pouring through the three high windows.

At the end and in front of a finely carved medieval

fireplace there was a tall, imposing-looking man whom she was sure was the Marquis.

For a moment she felt it was impossible to move towards him, and as if her feet were glued to the floor.

Then with an effort she walked forward and when she reached the Marquis dropped a small curtsy.

There was no doubt of the look of surprise on his face as he asked:

"You are the Miss Cavendish I was expecting?"

"Y . . yes . . My Lord."

It was an effort to speak, and as if he realised she was shy he said:

"I had the idea you would be older, and I think too I was expecting you to look like a Dutchwoman."

There was just a touch of amusement in his voice, and Lela forced a little smile to her lips.

"I am . . English . . My Lord."

"I was told you wanted to see me urgently, Miss Cavendish, and as the message came through the servants of Count Hans van Ruydaal, with whom I am staying, it was not very explicit."

"I asked to . . see you . . My Lord . . for a special . . reason," Lela said.

She was in fact upset and perturbed.

It had not been made clear to the Marquis, as she had expected, that she was bringing him a picture.

Then she was quick-brained enough to realise that Mr. Nijsted had said her visit was to be a secret.

Therefore, until she told the Marquis, it was obvious he would not know the reason.

Now he said:

"Please sit down, Miss Cavendish, and tell me what this is all about. Are you stranded in Amsterdam without any money, or perhaps you have been kidnapped by a Dutch pirate!"

He was talking to put Lela at her ease, but he was in fact astonished by her appearance.

He had been so sure when he had been told that an Englishwoman wished to see him urgently that it was the usual trouble.

Somebody stranded in a foreign country with no means of getting home.

Or else, as he had said jokingly, she had somehow become involved in a reprehensible manner with men from whom she could not escape.

He was aware that Lela was elegantly dressed and therefore unlikely to be penniless.

But he had never imagined that anybody could look so incredibly lovely, and at the same time so afraid.

It was obvious that something was very wrong.

As she sat down as he suggested on the sofa, he thought that it was a long time since he had seen a woman of any age who was so beautiful.

A connoisseur of beauty, he considered himself a judge of women, even though he despised them. He knew that Lela was a Lady.

Only good breeding could have produced such perfect features, such slim fingers, and such a high instep.

He was therefore extremely curious as to why she was here, and because she seemed almost incapable of speaking he said very gently:

"Now, what can I do for you?"

"I . . I have brought you . . a . . p . . picture, My Lord."

"A picture?"

This was something the Marquis had not expected.

Now he realised for the first time, because he had been looking at her face, that she carried a parcel under her right arm.

She held it out to him and he said:

"I suppose, because people talk, that you are aware I am here to buy pictures."

"I was .. told that .. My Lord," Lela said, "and I have .. therefore brought you a .. picture in which I .. think you .. might be .. interested."

"That is very kind of you," the Marquis said, "but I hope you will not be disappointed if it is something in which I am not interested."

Taking a deep breath, Lela looked away from him as she said:

"It is something .. unusual .. and I thought only you .. could help me."

The Marquis raised his eyebrows.

"If it is a question of a picture," he said, "I should have thought that almost everybody in Holland would be able to advise you on that subject!"

Lela clasped her fingers together.

"I am .. here because you are .. English, My Lord."

The Marquis had taken the picture from her, but he did not undo it. Instead he asked:

"What does that mean?"

"It means .. that I .. trust you."

The Marquis looked at her searchingly before he said:

"I find what you are saying a little difficult to understand."

As if she realised she was not telling the story as she should be, Lela said.

"My Aunt is the *Barones* van Alnradt, and her late husband was a close friend of Des Tombe."

She waited, thinking the Marquis must recognise the name, but he was only looking puzzled.

"Des Tombe .. who died recently," Lela explained quickly, 'was the gentleman who left Vermeer's *Head of a Girl* to the .. Mauritshuis."

"I have heard of that picture," the Marquis said, "and of course I must see it before I leave Holland."

"I am . . staying with . . my Aunt," Lela went on. "She is seriously ill, and it is . . important she should . . have a . . a very expensive operation."

Now there was a look in the Marquis's eyes as if he began to realise the point of the story.

But he did not say anything, and Lela continued:

"I was . . looking around the house to see if there was . . anything I could . . sell . . and I found what appears to be . . a sketch for Vermeer's portrait in . . one of the late *Baron*'s . . rooms."

"So that is what you have brought for me to see!" the Marquis said.

Lela had spoken so hesitatingly and with such shyness that he had had a little difficulty in following what she was saying.

Now he told himself it was because she was hoping he would buy the picture, and was therefore asking for money that she felt so embarrassed.

He undid the string with which she had tied the parcel up, and lifted out the picture.

The moment he looked at it he was thrilled by the beauty of the subject and the way in which it was painted.

The face of the girl looking over her shoulder, the enquiring expression in her brown eyes made, he thought, one of the most attractive pictures he had ever seen.

It was not completely finished.

But it was impossible for him not to realise how skilfully Vermeer had arranged his subject.

The light on the girl's face against the dark background, the blue of the ribbon which covered her forehead against her skin, and above all, a sense of reality which made the picture seem almost as if it spoke to him.

He stared at it for quite a long time before he asked:

"Who else has seen this picture?"

"N . . no one," Lela replied.

"You did not show it to your Aunt?"

"No . . she is . . very ill and if it is . . not, as I think, a sketch that Vermeer made . . before his . . finished work . . I would not . . wish to raise her . . hopes."

"I can understand your feeling like that," the Marquis said. "At the same time, it seems incredible that this sketch has not been seen before."

"I think," Lela said hesitatingly, trying to remember what Mr. Nijsted had said, "that the *Baron* was . . keeping it until . . his friend Des Tombe . . died and the Mauritshuis . . as had been arranged . . had received . . Vermeer's finished . . portrait."

"Yes, I can see the point of that," the Marquis agreed. "At the same time it seems to me extraordinary that no one, as you say, is aware of its existence."

Lela made a little gesture with her hands.

"Not as . . far as . . I know," she said. "Of course . . I have only just . . arrived in Holland to . . stay with my Aunt."

"And as you want to sell this sketch for her, what are you asking for it?" the Marquis enquired.

"I have . . no idea of its . . worth," Lela answered, "and that is why I have . . come to you. I am afraid that if I . . take it to the Dutch Dealers . . they might think . . because I am so young . . that they need not give me the right . . price."

She paused, then not looking at the Marquis in case he should see in her eyes that she was not speaking the truth, she said:

"I . . I thought that if you . . spoke to Mr. Nijsted . . who is . . I understand . . the Dealer who bought a . . number of pictures . . from the *Baron* he would not . . dare to deceive you . . or rather . . my Aunt . . as he might otherwise . . try to do."

"Nijsted?" the Marquis said, "I am sure that is the name of one of the Dealers I was told is honest. If moreover he knew the *Baron*, then of course it might make things easier for us both."

"Are you . . saying that you will . . buy the sketch?"

"Of course I will buy it," the Marquis said, "if it is what you say it is. And I promise you, Miss Cavendish, that I will pay what is a fair and just price."

"That is what I was . . sure you would say," Lela murmured.

"Because I am English?"

"Because you are a . . Gentleman," Lela said without thinking.

The Marquis laughed.

"That is a very disarming statement, and of course, like a real Gentleman, I will not try to cheat you."

Lela blushed, and it made her look very beautiful.

"I am sure . . My Lord . . you would not do that . . and now I can . . go home."

"Where are you staying?" the Marquis enquired.

"At The Hague with my Aunt."

"And you say she is very ill?"

"Very ill indeed . . and unless she has . . the operation immediately . . she may soon . . die."

"Then I promise I will make enquires about this sketch as quickly as I can."

"Thank you very . . very much . . I am very . . grateful!"

Lela had risen to her feet, and so did he.

For a moment they looked at each other.

She had the feeling that he was looking deep into her soul, and could see that she was trying to deceive him.

Because she was frightened, she said quickly:

"I . . I must go . . I want to get back to my . . Aunt."

"I can understand that," the Marquis said, "and I only hope I can be instrumental in helping her back to health."

They had reached the door.

As he opened it he saw Nanny sitting primly upright at the other end of the hall.

"I see you have somebody with you," he said.

"My old Nurse who came with me from England," Lela explained.

"May I say that I hope you will enjoy your stay in Holland, even though your Aunt is so ill."

"Thank you . . it is very beautiful . . and very . . exciting for me to be here," Lela said.

As she walked out into the hall she had a sudden thought and stepped backwards.

"There is . . something I . . must say," she said in a voice little above a whisper.

The Marquis was surprised as he had been following her from the room they had just left.

"You will not . . understand," Lela said, "but . . please . . when you return to England . . please do not tell anybody . . anybody at all . . that you have met me . . here in Holland."

She spoke in such an agitated way that the Marquis raised his eyebrows before he said:

"Am I to understand that this is a secret visit, or that you are in hiding?"

"Yes . . I am in . . hiding," Lela said, "and it is very . . important for me that nobody should . . know."

Once again she was looking at him pleadingly.

He thought he had never before seen such beautiful eyes that were so expressive.

"Then of course," he said with a smile, "I must once again behave like a Gentleman, and keep your secret!"

"Thank you . . thank you!" Lela said. "It was . . stupid of me . . not to . . mention it before."

Once again she moved into the hall, and now Nanny was waiting for her at the open door.

"Thank you very . . very much!" Lela said again, holding out her hand and curtsying as she did so.

The Marquis felt her fingers trembling in his and thought it strange that she was still so frightened.

As he watched her walk away he thought that no one could move more gracefully or, as she reached the door and glanced over her shoulder, look more lovely than the girl in the Vermeer portrait.

Then as they drove away and he saw her for a moment silhouetted against the water of the canal, he thought she could not be real.

He felt sure he must have dreamt this whole strange encounter.

But when he went back into the Sitting-Room, there was the Vermeer sketch lying on the chair where he had left it.

But instead of two brown eyes looking at him enquiringly, they were much larger and blue, while the small pointed face was framed by hair that was the colour of sunshine.

Chapter Five

Lela fortunately did not have to tell her Aunt she had been all the way to Amsterdam.

When she got back wondering what she should say, she found the *Barones* was fast asleep.

She had obviously taken the special pills which took away the pain, but also inevitably made her drowsy.

She therefore did not see the *Barones* until late in the evening.

After dinner when she went to her bedroom she found her awake, but still not thinking very clearly.

"Have you – been all right – my dearest child?" she asked.

"Yes, of course, Aunt Edith, and I am so sorry you are in pain."

"It has gone – now," the *Barones* said, "and tomorrow – we must have a – long talk – together. I have remembered – that I have some – souvenirs of your mother – which I am – sure you would – enjoy seeing."

"I would love that," Lela said.

Realising it was an effort for her Aunt to talk, she kissed her very gently, wished her goodnight and went downstairs to find a book to read.

It was too early to go to bed, and therefore she went to the bookshelves. There were large numbers of them in different rooms.

She then went to a window and opened it to look out over the garden.

The stars were coming out in the sky and it was all very quiet and extremely beautiful.

As she looked out, she was thinking of how interesting it had been to meet the Marquis and how handsome he was.

In fact he was the only man she had really admired since her father had died.

In contrast to the fathers of the girls with whom she had stayed when she was at School in Florence, her father had been a tall man.

In comparison the Italians had seemed small and insignificant.

Although when she was older they had paid her compliments, she had thought it was just their exaggerated way of speaking.

She had not been particularly interested in them.

But the Marquis was different.

There was something in his deep voice which made him seem very much a man.

Apart from that, he was very large and overwhelming in the small room in which they had talked.

She wished she had been able to discuss his horses with him and his home in England.

She had known when she was in Florence that she was homesick for the green of the English countryside, the ancient great houses, and the people whose blood was the same as her own.

"I would like to have known him better," she thought, but knew it was unlikely she would ever see him again.

Strangely enough, however, when she went to bed she dreamt about him.

Although in the morning she could not remember her dream at all clearly, she was vividly aware that she had been with him.

She felt as if she was still aware of his vibrations beside her.

When Nanny came to call her she said:

"It's going to be very hot today, Miss Lela, and I'm not walking all that way to the Museum in the heat!"

Lela was about to protest, then knowing Nanny was old and disliked walking, she said instead:

"Of course, Nanny, and we will not go out if it is too much for you. I will paint some of the flowers in the garden. I am sure Aunt Edith would like a picture of them when she wakes."

"Now that's what I call sensible!" Nanny said.

Lela found a small new canvas among the others in the *Baron*'s Studio, and taking her own paints she went into the garden.

The roses in their various different colours were very lovely.

She thought she would like to paint the tulips for which Holland was famous, then wondered nervously where she would be when Spring came and the tulips were in bloom.

As Nanny had said, it was very hot.

The sun finally drove her back into the house where she finished her picture upstairs in the Studio.

She glanced into her Aunt's bedroom to see if she was awake, but she was still asleep.

It was nearly luncheon time when Lela came down from the Studio to give her finished picture to her Aunt.

The *Barones* was sitting up in bed looking very pale and drawn.

Lela thought as she entered the room that if the Marquis did not buy her sketch soon, it would be too late.

Her Aunt however made a great effort to admire the picture she had painted for her, and complimented her on her style.

"You are a very clever artist, my dear," she said, "and I only wish you could have come here when your Uncle

95

was alive. He would have been delighted with your work!"

"Now you are paying me compliments I do not deserve!" Lela said. "His Studio is so beautifully arranged, and I think it was very clever of him to find so many canvasses of the different periods."

"I must confess," her Aunt answered, "that I find all those technicalities rather boring. As long as a picture is beautiful, I just want to look at it, and it really does not matter to me whether it was painted yesterday, or three hundred years ago!"

Lela laughed, and replied:

"I am sure you should not say things like that when you are living in Holland!"

"Of course not," the *Barones* agreed, "but they would understand me in England."

Lela went into the small Dining-Room to have her luncheon alone, and when she had finished Nanny came in to say:

"Your Aunt's going to sleep, so don't disturb her, and it's something I'm going to do too, and for that matter the rest of the people in the household."

She spoke a little aggressively as if she thought Lela would insist on going to the Museum.

Instead she said:

"You rest, Nanny, and I am going to read some of the interesting books I have seen in the Drawing-Room. Perhaps later, if it is cooler, we can go to the Mauritshuis."

She saw Nanny was pleased with her reply and went into the Drawing-Room where all the windows were open.

The doors had also been left open, and the scent of the flowers in the garden seemed to fill the house.

Most of the books, as she expected, were written in

Dutch, but there were also a number in French, and one or two novels in English.

Because she felt it was good to practise her French she picked up a novel by Guy de Maupassant.

Putting her feet up on the sofa she was soon absorbed in it.

It must have been an hour or so later when she heard somebody come into the room, and thought it was Nanny.

"Have you had a good sleep–?" she began.

Then she saw with surprise that it was not Nanny, but a strange young man, thick-set and not particularly good-looking.

In fact, he had the heavy, rather hard features of a Dutchman.

For a moment she just stared at him and he stared at her as if he was surprised to see her.

At last Lela rose to her feet saying:

"Good afternoon!"

She spoke in English, and the young man answered in the same language, but with a definite accent:

"Who are you? Why are you here?"

"I am a guest of the *Barones* van Alnradt," Lela said. "I am afraid you will not be able to see her as she is ill."

"I know that," the man replied, "and I am Nicolaes van Alnradt, the *Barones*'s Stepson."

Lela realised that this was the young man she had heard of from her Aunt, who was behaving badly and trying to sell the pictures that belonged to his brother.

She looked at him warily, then said:

"The *Barones* was my mother's sister, and I am her niece, Lela Cavendish."

"If that is who you are, you can give her a message!" Nicolaes van Alnradt said.

He looked round as he spoke.

Then he went across the room to where on the wall

was a beautiful picture by Hendrick Avercomo, of people skating on ice.

It was not very large, but exceedingly fine, and as he lifted it down Lela asked:

"What are you doing?"

"I am taking this picture because I consider it is mine."

"You cannot do that!" she exclaimed. "It is not yours . . it belongs to your brother!"

"What do you know about it?" he demanded. "Anyway, it is none of your business!"

"I will not let you steal my Aunt's pictures because she is too ill to stop you!" Lela cried. "Put that picture back at once! You had better leave this house, you have no right to be here!"

She spoke furiously and Nicolaes looked at her darkly, holding the picture in both hands.

"You are going to be difficult, are you?" he said. "Get out of my way or you will be sorry you interfered!"

"If you take that picture out of this house I shall immediately send for the Police!" Lela threatened.

She was standing between Nicolaes and the door.

She felt he was wondering if he could brush her aside and leave the room with the picture.

She was determined he should not do so.

She reached out and held onto the frame with both hands, trying to wrest it from him, and saying as she did so:

"You are behaving abominably! Go away, or I shall have to call the servants to stop you from stealing!"

She tugged at the picture as she spoke, and Nicolaes held it even tighter as he said:

"Get out of my way, you idiot little English girl! What the hell does it matter to you if I take the picture or not – unless you want it for yourself!"

"It belongs to my Aunt for her lifetime, after which it belongs to your brother!" Lela retorted.

She pulled again at the frame as she spoke.

Nicolaes taking one hand from the picture, hit out at her as hard as he could.

His fist struck her shoulder and she screamed.

After the Marquis had said goodbye to Lela the previous evening he had sat looking at the sketch she had left with him until the Count returned.

"Good news, Carew!" he exclaimed. "I have a magnificent picture by Van Der Velde arriving in an hour or so, and another by Jan Van de Cappelle."

"I am delighted," the Marquis replied. "But what do you think of this?"

The Count looked at the canvas he had beside him and exclaimed:

"The Vermeer there has been so much talk about! Who has copied it for you?"

"It is not a fake," the Marquis said, "but the original sketch painted by Vermeer before he produced his finished picture which is now in the Mauritshuis Museum."

"A sketch?" the Count exclaimed.

He picked up the picture, looked at it searchingly, then turned it over to look at the canvas.

"It certainly looks old," he said, "but who brought it to you?"

"A young girl who says she is the niece of the *Barones* van Alnradt."

The Count looked surprised.

"I knew the *Baron*, and the *Barones* for that matter. A charming couple, but after his death she appears to have gone into retirement."

"Apparently she is ill," the Marquis said, "and her niece wants to sell the picture to pay for a very serious operation."

"And she says it is an original sketch by Vermeer?"

"She thinks that the man who gave the *Head of a Girl* to the Mauritshuis was a friend of the *Baron*'s."

"I believe that is true," the Count remarked slowly, "but I cannot credit that this is really a sketch done by Vermeer. If such a sketch existed, we would surely have heard of it before now."

"That is what I thought myself," the Marquis said.

"It is certainly attractive," the Count conceded grudgingly, "but I should make very sure it is authentic before you waste a penny on it."

"That is exactly what I thought I should do," the Marquis agreed, "and Miss Cavendish suggested that I should get in touch with a dealer called Nijsted."

"I know of him," the Count said, "but I would not trust him very far, although that applies to quite a number of the Dealers. The pictures I have brought you have been authenticated by the top Director of the Rijksmuseum."

The Marquis laughed.

"You could not do better!"

"That was what I thought myself," the Count smiled.

"At the same time," the Marquis went on reflectively, "I feel sorry for Miss Cavendish. She is very concerned about her Aunt, and is actually an extremely pretty young girl!"

"Aha!" the Count exclaimed. "Now you will have to be more careful than ever! Buying pictures is one thing, but when a very pretty girl is concerned in the sale, it is always extremely risky!"

"You are a cynic!" the Marquis said.

"That accusation comes well from you," the Count retorted, "when you have been one for years!"

The Marquis knew this was true.

At the moment he was indeed cynical after the way he had been treated by the two women he was trying to forget.

Then he remembered Lela's blue eyes, and the

100

undoubted look of fear in them, and the way her hands had trembled.

"Why should she be so frightened?" he asked himself, as he had done ever since she had left him.

"Having told you the good news about your pictures," the Count said, "I also have some bad, although I hope you will not think it is very bad."

"What is that?" the Marquis asked.

"Her Majesty is already aware of your arrival," the Count replied, "and she has invited you to luncheon tomorrow at the *Huis ten Bosch*"

There was a pause before the Marquis managed to say:

"I am of course exceedingly honoured."

"It will not be as bad as you anticipate," the Count went on. "Her Majesty has a public appointment early in the afternoon, so luncheon is early and you will be able to escape immediately afterwards. She would however like to have a word with you before her other guests arrive."

"I hope you have accepted for me?" the Marquis said.

"Of course," the Count agreed, "and as I am not invited, I will be spending the time until you return seeking out more pictures of which there is no doubt as to their authenticity."

He looked at the Vermeer sketch as he spoke and the Marquis said:

"You do not think it possible that this is something that is really unique and has just been forgotten until now?"

"I think it so unlikely," the Count said, "that it might actually be true."

"Then how are we to prove it is not a fake?" the Marquis asked.

"I will take it to my friend at the Rijksmuseum," the Count replied, "but for Heaven's sake, Carew, do not mention it to any of the Dealers who are coming here later."

"Why not?" the Marquis enquired.

"Because, my dear friend, they will rush to The Hague and offer the *Barones* a dozen times more than she might expect to get, and blow up the discovery so that collectors from all over Europe will be competing with each other to own it."

"In other words, you are saying it is worth a great deal of money!" the Marquis said.

"*If* it is genuine," the Count replied, accentuating the first word.

"Very well," the Marquis agreed, "we will keep it a secret. But if I do buy it, I want to pay the girl a fair price because she needs it for her Aunt's operation."

"Another thing you should check," the Count said, "is if the *Barones* really needs one. It is the very old story of the dying father, mother or sister that wrings the heart of the ardent collector."

"Stop being so suspicious!" the Marquis exclaimed. "She is just a very young girl who would never deceive anybody!"

He spoke firmly, but he was aware that again he was asking himself the question: "Why was she so frightened?"

Then as the Count heard voices in the hall he realised the pictures he had selected for the Marquis and the Dealers who were bringing more had arrived.

He quickly picked up Lela's sketch and put it away in a cupboard.

The following morning the Marquis thought with satisfaction that he had bought three excellent Dutch pictures which would certainly interest the King, if no one else.

He was specially thrilled with the skating scene.

Of a very high quality, it inevitably demanded a very high price.

102

Then there were two others which would, he knew, fit perfectly into his Gallery.

He had spent a lot of money, but he knew he had paid less for them than he might have done in a Saleroom.

He was prepared to buy several more before he returned to England.

When the Count joined him for breakfast he told him that his fastest horses and lightest carriage were waiting to carry him to The Hague.

"I thought you might like to go early," he said, "and look in at the Mauritshuis before luncheon, and see Vermeer's original painting for yourself."

"That is what I have every intention of doing," the Marquis replied. "I have of course seen reproductions of it in the English newspapers and magazines, and I could hardly leave Holland without looking at the real thing!"

"You should also take the opportunity while you are in The Hague," the Count went on, "of calling on the *Barones* to see if she really is as ill as you have been led to believe."

"Still suspicious?" the Marquis teased. "Really, Hans, you should be a detective!"

"If you knew of the way a great number of the Dealers behave when there is a chance of making money," the Count said, "you would realise that in Holland we would be able to write a dozen detective stories every week!"

The Marquis was about to make some mocking reply.

Then he remembered that if it had not been for Willy, he would have been caught in a very humiliating position.

He personally had not had the slightest suspicion of what had been intended.

For a moment his eyes darkened, and his lips were set in a tight line.

As if he was aware that it was a sensitive subject, the Count began to talk about something quite different until the Marquis was ready to leave for The Hague.

He enjoyed driving in the carriage, not minding the heat, and finding the flat vista with its canals and windmills very attractive.

When he arrived at the Mauritshuis he walked through the galleries until he found the Vermeer.

He stood looking at the head of the Girl, realising the sketch Lela had brought him was a brilliant portrayal of the Master's work.

But as he gazed at it he found himself not thinking of brown eyes but again of two large blue ones that held an expression of fear in them.

Queen Wilhelmina was delighted to see the Marquis when he arrived at the *Huis ten Bosch*.

She began to reminisce over the time she had spent at Kyne, and how much she had enjoyed her visit.

She enquired about a large number of the Marquis's family, then asked;

"And when, My Lord, are you to be married? I am sure that Kyne needs a hostess."

"Perhaps that is true, Ma'am, but in the meantime I am enjoying my bachelorhood!," the Marquis replied with a smile.

"You should be thinking of the future," the Queen said firmly. "You need a son to inherit and to carry on your position at Court, and of course several daughters as attractive as your mother."

It was a subject in which the Marquis had no desire to be involved.

He was therefore relieved when his *tête-à-tête* with the Queen was interrupted by the other guests arriving for luncheon.

As he had anticipated, they were elderly Dutch Statesmen who could only talk on serious subjects and seldom laughed.

Because Her Majesty had an appointment as he had

been told, the meal was short, and when she said goodbye to the Marquis, the Queen said:

"I am sorry I have to leave, and I can only hope, My Lord, that you will visit me again before you leave Holland."

"I shall be very honoured Ma'am if you permit me to do so," the Marquis replied.

The Queen hurried away, and he too was able to leave.

It was still early in the afternoon, and he had thought on his way to The Hague that the Count had been sensible in suggesting that he should call on the *Barones*.

The coachman found the way to the house and as they drew up outside it the footman got down to ring the bell.

As the man did so, the Marquis saw that the front door was open.

After waiting a few minutes with no servant appearing, he walked into the hall.

It was cool after the burning brilliance of the sunshine.

He was just wondering where he might find Lela when he heard a scream.

The sound came from behind a door on the other side of the hall and without hesitating the Marquis opened it and walked into the room.

To his astonishment, he saw Lela clutching the frame of a picture with both hands while a thick-set young man was striking at her with his fist.

He aimed for her face, but she ducked behind the picture.

Nicolaes struck her on the shoulder as he had done before. She screamed a second time.

The Marquis strode towards them.

"What the devil is going on here?" he demanded.

Neither Nicolaes nor Lela had heard him enter the room, and now they both stared at him in astonishment.

Because he was so large and overpowering, Nicolaes instinctively let go of the picture.

Lela who had been pulling at it with all her strength stumbled and fell to the floor.

"How dare you strike a woman!" the Marquis said before Nicolaes could speak. "Get out before I knock you down!"

The manner in which he spoke and the fact that he was so much bigger made the Dutchman feel that it would be hopeless to ignore so definite a command.

As he turned and went from the room the Marquis did not even bother to watch him go, but bent to pick up Lela from the floor.

She was so relieved that Nicolaes had gone that she ignored the picture and held onto the Marquis.

"Thank you . . thank . . you!" she cried. "You came . . just at the right . . moment!"

He kept his arm around her until she was steady on her feet.

Then as she put her hand to her shoulder where Nicolaes had struck it the Marquis asked:

"Has that man hurt you? What were you doing and why should he strike you?"

"H . . He is Nicolaes van Alnradt, my Aunt's younger Stepson," Lela managed to explain. "He was . . trying to . . steal one of the pictures that . . belong to my Aunt . . until she dies. . . and then to his brother."

Because she no longer seemed to need his assistance, the Marquis bent down and picked up the picture.

Its skating scene was rather like the one he had just bought, and was just as beautifully painted.

He laid it against a chair.

Then he turned to find Lela had sat down on the sofa as if her legs would no longer support her.

She was still rubbing her shoulder and he guessed it was very painful.

"Surely," he said, "there should be somebody here to

106

guard these pictures which I can see are very valuable. Where are the servants?"

"They are all . . resting . . because it is . . so hot," Lela replied, "and I . . was reading when he . . came into the room."

"And your Aunt is upstairs?" the Marquis asked.

"Like everybody else in the house, she is asleep," Lela replied, "and I suppose Nicolaes thought he could . . steal the picture . . at a time . . when nobody could be . . quite sure who had . . taken it."

"It is utterly despicable!" the Marquis exclaimed. "You must tell the servants in future to keep the door shut and locked, so that nobody can just walk in."

"I suppose leaving it open is . . something . . they have . . always done when the . . weather is so hot."

"Then it is something that must be stopped!" the Marquis said.

He sat down on the sofa beside her.

He thought as she looked at him gratefully that her eyes were even more beautiful than they had seemed yesterday.

She was in fact so lovely that it was hard to believe she was real, and not some figment of his imagination.

"Tell me about yourself," he said. "Yesterday you were very mysterious, and I found myself wondering why you are hiding in Holland, and from whom?"

"You . . promised not to . . speak of it when you . . return to England," Lela reminded him quickly.

"I always keep my promises," the Marquis replied loftily, "but I would like you to trust me."

He knew as he spoke that he had made a mistake because Lela looked away from him.

He was certain she was telling herself that on no account must she confide in somebody she had only just met, and who was also an Englishman.

"I went this morning to see Vermeer's *Head of a Girl* in the Mauritshuis."

"It is lovely . . is it not?" Lela asked.

There was a little pause, then she asked hesitatingly:

"Have you . . decided to . . buy the . . sketch?"

"Of course I will buy the sketch, if it is genuine," the Marquis replied.

He was watching Lela's face as he spoke, but she rose to her feet and walked across the room to stand at the window.

The sunshine turned her hair to gold.

He thought her profile silhouetted against the trees outside was more beautiful than anything a Dutch Master had ever portrayed on canvas.

In a voice he could hardly hear she said after a moment:

"Aunt Edith is . . very ill and . . unless she has an operation she will . . d . . die!"

"I understand," the Marquis said, "and I will give you my decision tomorrow."

Lela turned to the window.

"Please," she begged, "please buy it . . if she does die . . it will be so . . terrible. She has to wait . . too long just to prevent her . . Stepson, whom you saw just now, from stealing everything he can lay his hands on!"

"Surely," the Marquis asked, "there is somebody who could prevent him from doing so?"

"Only his brother . . and he is . . in Java."

The Marquis's lips tightened.

"I can see your problem, Miss Cavendish. The only thing I can suggest is that you go ahead with your Aunt's operation, and whether the picture is genuine or not, I will gladly pay what it costs."

Lela gave a little cry.

"That is . . kind and very . . generous of you," she said, "but of course . . my Aunt would not . . accept that. She would not wish to ask for charity . . and that is what it . . would be . . if she could give you . . nothing in . . return."

As she spoke she thought perhaps she was making a mistake.

At the same time, she knew her mother and father would be shocked at her accepting the assistance of a stranger just because it was a "hard luck" story.

"I think you are sacrificing your Aunt for an unnecessary scruple," the Marquis said. "Supposing I talk to her and suggest, because she is English, as I am, that I wish to be of assistance?"

Lela drew in her breath.

"How could . . anybody be . . so kind . . so wonderful?" she asked.

She moved as she spoke towards the Marquis, who was sitting on the sofa.

As she reached him her eyes met his and it seemed as if neither of them could look away.

Then as he did not speak, Lela said looking at the clock:

"Aunt Edith usually sleeps until about three o'clock, but if that is too long to ask you to wait, I will wake her now."

"No, no, of course not!" the Marquis said. "I can easily wait until three o'clock, and I suggest while we do so that you sit down and tell me about yourself, which I would find very interesting."

"I cannot think . . why," Lela replied, "when you must have so many other interests."

The Marquis smiled and asked:

"Tell me about your father and mother."

Because it was a subject on which Lela was always willing to talk, she told him how brave her father had been, and how he had won the Victoria Cross.

Then she told him how beautiful her mother had been.

"And I suppose you are very like her?" the Marquis remarked.

"I am always flattered when I am told that I am," Lela replied, "but Mama was far more beautiful than I could ever be!"

She spoke so naturally that, while the Marquis thought it would be impossible for anyone to be more beautiful than she was, he did not say so.

Instead he persuaded Lela to tell him of the house in which they had lived in the country until her father was killed.

"What happened after that?" he enquired.

To his surprise she lapsed into silence, then after a moment she looked at the clock on the mantelpiece.

"Aunt Edith should be . . awake in another five minutes," she said.

"You are being evasive," the Marquis said, "and you are hiding something from me."

She did not answer, and he said:

"Can you imagine how infuriating it is for a man to be confronted by a problem which he has no possibility of solving, but which is persistently there in his mind?"

Lela gave a little nervous laugh.

"I am sure, My Lord, you have much more . . interesting things to . . occupy your time . . than me."

If the question had come from any other woman, the Marquis knew there would have been a flirtatious look in her eyes, and he would be expected to make the obvious answer.

But again Lela was so natural and so unspoilt.

He therefore had no intention of paying her the type of compliment which he knew instinctively she would not expect or understand.

Instead he asked:

"Is this your first journey abroad?"

"Oh no," Lela replied, "Mama sent me to a Finishing

School in Florence, then when she died just before I was coming home, I stayed on for another year until I was out of mourning, and studied Art with a teacher at the Uffizi Gallery."

The Marquis's shrewd mind found it difficult to understand.

How, when she had spoken of how poor they were, after the death of her father, was she able to attend a Finishing School in Florence.

His brain also registered the fact that she had studied Art at the most important Gallery in Florence.

Lela was simultaneously aware that she had made a mistake in telling him that.

Quickly, because she was nervous that he might suspect that she herself had painted the Vermeer sketch, she got to her feet.

"I am sure Aunt Edith will be awake now," she said.

As she spoke, the door opened and Geetruida burst into the room.

"Miss Lela – come quickly!"

"What is it, Geetruida?"

"The mistress – I think – I'm afraid – she is dead!"

Lela ran to the door and as Geetruida hurried ahead of her up the stairs she followed her and the Marquis did the same.

They reached the landing and Geetruida pushed open the door into the *Barones's* room.

She had obviously called her mistress and drawn back the curtains before she moved to the bed to look at her.

The sunshine was coming in through the windows and Lela could see her Aunt's face, very pale against the pillows.

Her eyes were closed and she might have been asleep except that there was a stillness about her which made it obvious she was not just unconscious, but no longer breathing.

One hand with its long thin fingers lay still on top of the sheet.

When Lela ran to her bedside to touch it, it was as cold as ice.

It was then she turned blindly away, as if she could not bear the sight, to find the Marquis just behind her.

Instinctively, like a child, she hid her face against his shoulder, and he put his arms around her.

She was not crying, but he could feel her body trembling against his.

"She did not suffer," he said gently in his deep voice.

Geetruida with tears running down her cheeks had gone from the room to find the other servants.

The Marquis and Lela did not move.

He just held her close against him, seeing the faint resemblance in the dead woman's face to the girl who seemed part of the sunshine and was youth and life itself.

Then there was the sound of voices and footsteps coming up the stairs.

With an effort Lela moved, and he knew that she was fighting for self-control.

"It is all right," he said very quietly, "and I will take you back to England."

Chapter Six

From then, as Lela thought afterwards, the Marquis simply took over.

She was feeling so stunned at the shock of finding her Aunt dead that she found it impossible to think clearly.

At the same time, it needed a tremendous effort to prevent herself from crying.

Her mother had always said that it was vulgar to cry in public, and she clenched her fingers together, trying to suppress the tears in her eyes.

While Geetruida and the other servants were weeping copiously, the Marquis started to give orders.

He sent a manservant immediately to fetch the Doctor and the Undertaker, and Geetruida was told to contact the *Barones's* Solicitor.

Then he took Lela to the Sitting-Room and said to her in his quiet, deep voice:

"I know that you will be worried about your Aunt's pictures, so I am now going to the Mauritshuis to see the Director."

Lela looked at him in surprise, and he realised she did not understand.

"I know that the pictures, which I can see are valuable, will be safe there, and I am sure I can persuade the Director to take charge of them until *Baron* Johan arrives from Java."

Lela did not speak and he went on:

113

"In the meantime the doors must be kept locked, and nobody except the people I have sent for are to be allowed in."

"Thank . . you," Lela said in a very small voice.

The Marquis drove off to the Mauritshuis and found that the Director of the Museum was on the premises.

He introduced himself and said:

"I have come to you, *Mijnheer*, with a difficult problem which I hope you can help me to solve."

"I will certainly do my best," the Director replied.

"After I had luncheon with Her Majesty the Queen," the Marquis said, "I thought I would call on the *Barones* van Alnradt, who is of the same nationality as myself."

The Director nodded, and the Marquis continued:

"I found on my arrival that a very valuable picture belonging to the old *Baron*'s collection was being removed from the house by Nicolaes van Alnradt."

He saw by the expression on the Director's face that Nicolaes's reputation was known to him.

He continued:

"I prevented him from stealing the picture, but I feel sure that once he is aware that his Step-mother is dead, he will return."

"I am therefore going to ask you," the Marquis went on, "if you would be kind enough to take charge of this collection of pictures and keep them in the Museum until their rightful owner, the *Baron* Johan van Alnradt, returns from Java."

The Director looked surprised, and the Marquis said quickly in case he refused:

"Of course, I could approach her Majesty on the matter, but I thought it would be a mistake when, as you know, she is so busy."

This proved to be the trump-card, and the Director said immediately:

"Of course, My Lord, I shall be only too happy to

accommodate the late *Baron*'s collection until his elder son returns."

"Thank you very much," the Marquis said, "I am exceedingly grateful. If you can spare the men and the vehicles necessary, I am sure they should be removed at once."

The Marquis departed, leaving the Director feeling as if he had somehow encountered a typhoon.

Before he left the house for the Museum, the Marquis had said to Nanny, who was the only one of the household who was not weeping:

"I suggest you pack your mistress's clothes immediately, for I think it would be a mistake for her to stay here."

Nanny looked at him in surprise, but she knew the voice of authority when she heard it.

When the Marquis arrived back, practically everything Lela possessed was already in her trunks.

He found her still in the Sitting-Room where he had left her, and she jumped up eagerly when he came into the room.

She looked very pale but, although he guessed she had cried when she was alone, she was now completely composed.

"You are . . back!" she said breathlessly.

"Yes, I am back," he said, "and I suggest I take you with me to Amsterdam."

She looked at him wide-eyed, and he said:

"I think it would be a mistake for you to stay here, for although I have arranged for the pictures to be removed to the Mauritshuis for safekeeping, that offensive young man may decide to return."

He saw Lela shiver, and knew that although there were servants in the house to protect her she would be apprehensive.

"What I am going to suggest," the Marquis said, "is

that you and Nanny go aboard my yacht which is in the Heerengracht Kanaal."

There was silence before Lela said hesitatingly:

"You .. you do not think I .. should attend Aunt Edith's Funeral?"

"That of course is for you to decide. At the same time, you told me you are in hiding, and the *Baron*, when he was alive, was a very distinguished man."

There was no need to say any more.

Lela realised immediately the implications of her Aunt's death being reported in the Dutch newspapers.

Since she was English, there would doubtless also be an account of her Funeral in *The Times* and *The Morning Post*.

In that case Sir Robert would see it, and he would be astute enough to guess where she was hiding herself.

"Y .. you are .. right," she said in a very small voice. "I .. cannot stay here .. and perhaps I should .. go back to England."

"I think that would be the sensible thing to do," the Marquis agreed. "Now get your hat and, as soon as you are ready, we will leave for Amsterdam."

He thought as Lela left the room that he had become very much more involved in her affairs than he had ever intended.

And yet, he asked himself, what else could he do?

There was not only the danger which might come from Nicolaes van Alnradt.

He knew Lela, who was so young, so unspoilt and innocent, would encounter danger from almost every man she met.

She was not only so lovely; there was something pure and untouched about her which the Marquis knew from past experience most men found irresistible.

"I will take her to England with me," he told himself, "and she must have relatives who will look after her."

He then called the servants in the house together.

He told them they could expect at any moment a van or perhaps two from the Mauritshuis Museum who would take the pictures away for safekeeping.

"Until they arrive," he said, "you must understand that the doors are to be kept locked, and no one except the Doctor and the Undertaker are to be allowed into the house. Then later there will be the *Baron*'s Solicitor, whom I am sure you all know by sight.

"We will do exactly as you say, My Lord," Geetruida said, and the other servants made the same promise.

Lela's trunks were being strapped to the back of the carriage which had brought the Marquis to The Hague, when two vans, each drawn by two sturdy horses, were waiting to draw up outside the front door.

Because he felt the servants might not have any spare money, the Marquis tipped the men who had come from the Museum before he left.

Lela thought it very kind and thoughtful of him.

She told herself that no other man could have been so wonderful as both to rescue her from the thieving Nicolaes and also to save the pictures.

Above all the Marquis had saved her from being found by her Stepfather.

She shuddered as she thought how frightening it would have been if he had turned up unexpectedly at the Funeral, and perhaps brought Mr. Hopthorne with him.

While she was putting on her hat and Nanny was finishing the hand-luggage, the old maid announced:

"I don't know if I'm on my head or my heels, and that's the truth!"

"His Lordship is taking us to his yacht, Nanny," Lela explained, "and we must now think of somewhere in England where we can be safe from Step-Papa."

"I thought we were safe here for at least a month or two," Nanny murmured.

"So did I," Lela agreed, "but how could we have guessed that poor Aunt Edith was so . . desperately ill?"

Her voice broke on the last words and Nanny said sharply:

"Now, don't you go upsetting yourself, Miss Lela. Your Aunt's in Heaven with your mother and they wouldn't want you looking like a ghost, and gentlemen hate women who cry their eyes out!"

"I will try . . not to do . . that," Lela said, "but it has all happened so . . suddenly!"

"I know, I know," Nanny said, "but perhaps it's all for the best! We're English, and that's where we belong. All we've got to do now is to think where we can go."

"That is easier said than done," Lela wanted to reply.

A servant came to carry down the hand-luggage.

Although she had no wish to keep the Marquis waiting, Lela went first to her Aunt's bedroom.

The Undertaker and the woman who laid out the dead had already been and had left her with her hands crossed on her breast.

Lela stood looking at her, then she went down on her knees.

She prayed that she would be reunited not only with her husband whom she had loved, but also with her mother and other members of her family.

It was a very sincere prayer, and she added a little one for herself.

"Please take . . care of me," she said, "and perhaps you and Mama will . . prevent my Stepfather from . . finding me . . and forcing me to . . marry a man I do not love. Help me . . help me . . as I am so alone . . and I am . . frightened!"

She bent her head and shut her eyes while she was praying, and suddenly she thought there was a brilliant light in the room.

It was not sunlight, but something far more vivid.

118

It was just a fleeting impression, and was at once gone, but she felt her prayer had been heard, and she no longer felt so afraid.

She ran down the stairs to where the Marquis was waiting for her.

As he saw her he thought with her fair hair and her blue eyes, she looked like the Goddess of Spring.

Lela said goodbye to the servants, and Geetruida cried again because she was leaving them.

Then she stepped into the carriage and sat on the back-seat beside the Marquis, while Nanny sat opposite them on the small seat.

"These are very fine horses," the Marquis said, "and I am sure I came to The Hague from Amsterdam in record time."

"My father used to try to break records when he drove in his carriage," Lela said, "but our horses were not particularly well-bred, and I am afraid he usually was disappointed."

The Marquis told her about the horses he had at Kyne, and especially a stallion with which he had won a number of Steeplechases.

He found that Lela was not only an attentive listener, but she knew quite a lot about horses and asked intelligent questions.

He was well aware that women like Lady Burton only went riding in the Park because it was fashionable to do so.

They knew very little about horses, except that they wished to be mounted on one that gave them as little trouble as possible.

He felt sure that, fragile and ethereal though she looked, Lela was a good horsewoman.

He was aware it was something that could not be taught but came from a natural ability and a love of the animal itself.

When they were not talking about horses, Lela admired the windmills.

The Marquis told her how they regulated the volume of water in the canals, and he found that surprisingly she was really interested in what he had to say.

In fact the journey seemed to pass very quickly.

Then they were driving through the streets of Amsterdam towards the Heerengracht Kanaal.

He was not surprised when Lela made exclamations of astonishment at the beauty of the houses.

"I thought you would appreciate them," he said. "This is the most beautiful canal in the whole of Amsterdam, and I think the finest house is the one in which I am staying with my friend Count Hans van Ruydaal."

"Then you are not staying on your yacht?" Lela asked.

"No, I am with my friend," the Marquis replied. "For tonight you and Nanny will be alone on the *Heron*, and we will leave for England tomorrow."

He was aware that a shadow passed over Lela's face.

It made him even more anxious to know why she was afraid of returning to England.

He wondered if her fear was of some man.

He found himself thinking he would like to kill anyone who could frighten anything so fragile and lovely.

He had not forgotten his fury at seeing Nicolaes van Alnradt striking Lela.

He told himself it was a natural reaction that any decent man would feel at seeing a blow struck at a woman.

But he knew it was something more than that.

They drove down the side of the canal, then as they passed the Count's house, the Marquis saw him standing in the open doorway.

It was obvious he was surprised at seeing that the Marquis was not alone, and that his carriage did not stop but went on to the end of the canal where the *Heron* was moored.

120

The yacht was looking very attractive with the white ensign flying from her stern.

Lela gazed enraptured.

"It is much bigger than I expected," she said. "It must be very exciting to have a ship all of your own."

"I am sure you will find it is quite comfortable," the Marquis replied.

They went aboard and the Marquis introduced them to the Captain and told him at the same time that they were to leave for England the next morning.

He showed Lela the Saloon, which she thought pretty.

He then took her below to show her the cabins which she and Nanny would occupy on the voyage.

"I have never been in a yacht before," Lela said, "and I feel it will be like a magical Doll's House!"

The Marquis laughed.

It struck him that it would be very amusing to show Lela a great many things she had never seen before, and perhaps a number of places.

Then he reminded himself severely that he disliked women.

He was only doing his duty in taking the girl, who was little more than child, back to England.

When they went back to the Saloon, they found Count Hans van Ruydaal there.

"I thought you must be running away from me, Carew!" he said.

The Marquis looked amused, knowing that he had followed them really because he was curious.

Now as he introduced Count Hans he said to Lela:

"Count Hans has been a most hospitable host while I have been in Holland."

The Count held out his hand.

"I heard you were staying with your Aunt," he said. "But why are you leaving Holland so quickly?"

"The *Barones* died this morning," the Marquis

explained before Lela could speak, "and Miss Cavendish has been very distressed by various things that have happened while she has been at The Hague."

"I am extremely sorry to hear that," the Count said quickly, "and even sorrier to hear that you are both leaving."

"I am sorry too," the Marquis replied, "but in fact, thanks to you, I have acquired what I came for."

"It is not a lot," the Count admitted, "but I have two more pictures waiting for you at the house which I think you will appreciate."

"I will come and look at them," the Marquis said.

He was aware as he spoke that while Hans was talking to him he was looking at Lela as if he could hardly believe his eyes.

Then the Count said:

"I think it would be extremely remiss if I did not ask Miss Cavendish to dine with us tonight. I have, as it happens, already invited a friend of mine who wishes to meet you, and it will certainly complete the party if Miss Cavendish will join us also."

The Marquis saw Lela first look excited by the idea, then as she thought perhaps it was incorrect for her to accept such an invitation, she looked at the Marquis.

He knew without her saying anything that she was afraid of making a social error.

At the same time, she did not want to be alone without him there to protect her.

"I think that is an excellent idea, Hans!" he said to the Count. "Perhaps your carriage could pick Miss Cavendish up a quarter-of-an-hour before we dine."

"That is what I was going to suggest," the Count said reproachfully, as if he thought the Marquis was telling him how to behave.

Then he said to Lela in a very different voice:

"Please dine with me! I want you to see my pictures,

122

but I assure you I possess nothing as beautiful as you are yourself!"

The Marquis felt annoyed, thinking it was a mistake for the Count to compliment her in the way he would have spoken to an older woman.

He walked towards the door of the Saloon.

"Come along, Hans," he said, "I will have plenty of time to see the pictures you have for me before I change for dinner. And as you yourself have pointed out, it is always a mistake to be too hasty when it concerns pictures!"

The Count however had taken Lela's hand in his.

"I will be counting the minutes until I see you again!" he said.

Lela blushed as the Count raised her hand and for a moment his lips touched the softness of her skin.

Then he followed the Marquis who was already climbing into the carriage, the coachman having turned the horses at the end of the canal.

As they drove away, the Marquis said sharply:

"Miss Cavendish is very young and very unsophisticated. It would be a mistake, Hans, to frighten her."

"Frighten her?" the Count asked in surprise. "I have never met a woman yet who was frightened by a compliment!"

"Then I must assure you that Miss Cavendish is very easily frightened," the Marquis said.

He spoke so aggressively that his friend looked at him in surprise.

Then suddenly he laughed.

"So the wind sits in that direction," he said, "and it is a question of 'Hands off!' I am sorry, Carew, but I believed you when you said you were fed up with women!"

"It is nothing like that!" the Marquis said sharply. "It

is just that I have to do my duty towards an Englishwoman in distress."

"I consider 'duty' a very inadequate word where that glorious Springlike creature is concerned!" the Count retorted irrepressibly.

It was then the Marquis was surprised by suddenly and unaccountably feeling angry with a friend whose company in the past he had always enjoyed.

On the yacht Lela was wondering if she was doing something very unconventional and wrong in going out to dinner the very day her Aunt had died.

She knew however that if she sat alone in the yacht she would feel rather frightened and very miserable.

It would be difficult not to keep worrying and worrying over what she should do when she reached England.

"The Marquis is so kind," she told herself. "I am sure I should take his advice and go home."

She thought too that what money she and Nanny had would last longer in England than it would in The Hague, if they had to pay for their accommodation.

She had of course no idea where to find cheap lodgings.

She tried to think of her father and mother's friends at home in the country, and wondered if she could beg any of them to hide her.

At the same time, she had the uncomfortable feeling that because Sir Robert was so rich, they would think she was only being tiresome and very ungrateful in refusing to do what he wished.

"What can we do, Nanny?" she asked as she washed and changed into an evening-gown.

"I wish I knew, Dearie," Nanny answered. "I've been puzzling my head ever since we left your Aunt's house as to where we could be safe."

"There must be somewhere!" Lela said pathetically.

"We'll just have to trust in God," Nanny said, "or

perhaps His Lordship has a cottage where no one would find us."

Lela's eyes lit up.

"That is a splendid idea, Nanny!" she exclaimed. "I cannot imagine why I did not think of that!"

At the same time she felt it was rather embarrassing to foist herself on the Marquis when he had already done so much for her.

She thought too it would be a mistake to discuss the subject with him until just before they arrived in England.

The Count's carriage was waiting for Lela and drove her the short distance to his house.

As she stepped out the Marquis was waiting at the top of the steps to greet her.

"You are very punctual, unlike most women!" he remarked.

"Mama said it was rude to be late . . and also I am hungry!" Lela replied.

The Marquis laughed.

He led her into the Sitting-Room where the visitor whom the Count had invited especially for him had already arrived.

She was in fact a very attractive Frenchwoman, married to a Dutch Diplomat who was at this moment on a visit to Germany.

She was not really beautiful, but she had a fascination that was very French.

She was dressed with a *chic* which labelled her gown as having definitely come from Paris.

It was impossible for her to talk to any man without subtly flirting with him with her eyes, her lips and every movement of her body.

She had already done her best to enslave the Marquis, for whom, she realised, the Count had invited her.

When Lela came into the room, both the Marquis and

the Count felt that she was the personification of Youth, and seemed to bring the sunshine with her.

She looked in wide-eyed admiration at the French *Vicomtesse*, and was far too innocent to understand the *double entendre* in almost everything she said.

And yet the Marquis thought with amusement that it would be impossible for any man at the dinner-table, not to find his eyes turning to Lela, although the sophisticated woman was giving what was a performance in the art of seduction.

They talked, they laughed, and although Lela did not understand everything that was said, she felt happy because the Marquis was there.

For the moment she could forget to be afraid about the future.

After dinner they all moved into the Sitting-Room, French fashion, with the gentlemen not remaining behind to drink alone.

Then the Marquis said to Lela:

"I was wondering if, amongst your other talents, you are a pianist?"

"I play a little," she answered.

"Then I suggest you see what you can do on that very impressive instrument in the corner of the room."

It was a fine piano, which the Count admitted he had been given by his mother, although it was seldom played except by visitors.

Lela ran her fingers over the keys.

The Marquis knew he had been right in thinking she not only had an artistic eye, but also musical skill.

He had suggested she should play because he felt she was bewildered by most of the conversation to which she had been listening.

He was not surprised when the *Vicomtesse* seated herself beside him.

She flirted with him in a low voice which, before he

had become disillusioned in women, he would have found extremely alluring.

Now he was aware that he was irritated by the fact that the Count was sitting by the piano, watching Lela.

There was an expression on his face which told the Marquis very clearly exactly what he was feeling about her.

"Dammit all, he should leave the girl alone! She is too young!" he said to himself.

He realised that the *Vicomtesse* was looking at him reproachfully because he had not heard what she had said.

Lela played first a Nocturne by Chopin, then some soft, romantic music by Strauss.

She was thinking as she played how handsome the Marquis looked, and could not help wondering what the *Vicomtesse* was saying to him.

She thought the Frenchwoman was exactly the type of person who would amuse him and that he must be very bored with somebody like herself.

He was only being kind to her because she was English.

"He is not only handsome and very grand," she thought, "he is also so clever that he most find me very dull, since I know nothing about the things which interest him, except for horses and pictures."

She did not understand why she suddenly felt depressed, and thought it must be because she was tired.

It had been a very upsetting day.

Nanny had exclaimed with horror when she undressed her and saw the heavy bruise on her shoulder where Nicolaes had struck her twice.

Lela knew that by this time it would gradually be turning black.

She was only thankful he had not hit her in the face, as he had intended. At the same time it was growing more and more painful even to play the piano.

She finished the piece and rose a little uncertainly to her feet.

"Please go on playing," the Count begged. "I am charmed by your music, as I am charmed by you."

He spoke in a low voice so that the Marquis and the *Vicomtesse* would not overhear, but Lela moved away from him and said to the Marquis:

"Please . . although it has been a . . lovely evening . . I think now I should go . . back to the yacht."

The Marquis got to his feet.

"I am sure you are right, and you must be very tired. I will take you back."

"N . . no . . please . . I can manage quite well . . alone," Lela said.

The Marquis ignored her protest and said to the Count:

"Is your carriage outside, Hans?"

"Of course!" he replied.

Lela said goodnight to the *Vicomtesse*, then thanked the Count very prettily.

"I will try to see you again tomorrow – if His Lordship does not spirit you away to England!" he said.

He moved a little closer to her as he added:

"I shall never forget you, and I hope I may come and see you when I am next in England."

"Thank . . you," Lela said, knowing she had no address to leave with him.

She turned towards the door and the Marquis followed her into the hall.

"I do not wish to . . take you away from . . your friends," she said in a low voice. "I shall be . . quite all right on my own."

"I am coming with you!" he said firmly.

He took her wrap from the servant who was holding it, and put it round her shoulders.

Then he helped her down the steps and into the carriage.

She wondered why she felt a sudden little thrill run through her because he was touching her.

Then as she got into the carriage and they were side by side, she wished it was not such a short distance to the yacht.

She wanted to talk to him as she had not been able to do all the evening.

She did not understand her own feelings, she only knew it was wonderful that he was there, and she wanted to be with him.

The yacht looked very romantic with its lights reflected on the water of the canal, and the moonlight was seeping through the leaves of the trees overhead.

Lela got out of the carriage and she expected the Marquis would say goodnight to her, and leave her to step up the gangplank alone.

Instead he said to the coachman:

"I will walk back, you need not wait."

Lela felt a little leap of her heart that he was not leaving her immediately.

She looked up at him pleadingly.

He thought, with the yacht behind her, its lights reflected in the canal and the stars overhead, it was a picture no artist could portray adequately on canvas.

For a long moment they paused, looked at each other and the moonlight seemed to be saying words they did not speak.

Then with an effort Lela turned and walked aboard the yacht and into the Saloon.

The Marquis followed her.

"You have had a long day," he said, "and I want to tell you that I think you have behaved with great courage. I know your father would have been proud of you."

Because he spoke so kindly, Lela felt the tears prick her eyes, and she said in a very low voice:

"That is a . . wonderful thing for . . you to . . say to

me . . and I know Papa would be very . . grateful that you have been so . . kind and . . understanding."

The Marquis sat down in one of the comfortable chairs.

Because she realised he was not leaving her straight away she sat down near him throwing off her wrap as she did so.

Her gown was an extremely pretty one that she had bought in Florence, and made her look very young.

It also accentuated the curves of her body and her small waist.

"I have been wondering, Lela," the Marquis said after a moment, "what I should do about you when we reach England."

"I . . I shall be . . all right," Lela said quickly.

She was determined that she must not be an encumbrance on him.

"What were you thinking tonight when the Count was paying you such extravagant compliments," the Marquis asked unexpectedly, "and made you feel shy?"

"When I . . stayed with my . . School-friends in their homes . . their brothers sometimes . . paid me . . compliments . . but because they were Italians . . they did not . . somehow seem . . real."

"And you thought the Count was the same?" the Marquis asked sharply.

Lela was silent for a moment as if he had set her a problem. Then she replied:

"They were . . real . . but somehow . . contrived . . as if he had said them . . many times before."

The Marquis laughed, and it was a spontaneous sound.

He had not expected Lela to say anything so perceptive, or understand what he knew was in fact the truth.

"Wherever you go," he said, "you are going to find that men will pay you compliments. That is why, Lela, you must tell me before we reach England exactly what has frightened you, and why you ran away."

130

He saw Lela's blue eyes widen, and knew that once again she was afraid, but he went on:

"You cannot expect me just to put you down on English soil and forget about you. If you do not wish to go to your own relatives, I might find one of mine who would be pleased to chaperon you, and introduce you to the Social World in which I know you would shine."

Lela drew in her breath.

"It is very . . kind of . . you . . My Lord . . but . . that is completely out of the . . question!"

"Why?" the Marquis asked.

"Because I have to hide! I cannot go . . anywhere in public! Your relatives would obviously want to . . know more about me . . and that has to . . remain a secret."

The Marquis leaned back in his chair.

"Now let us be sensible about this," he said. "Tell me what is upsetting you, and then I shall know how best I can find a solution because, although you may think otherwise, there is always a solution to every problem."

"N . . not . . mine," Lela said with a little sob.

"Tell me," the Marquis pleaded.

She made a sound that was almost a cry, then unexpectedly she moved from her chair and onto her knees beside him.

She looked up at him pleadingly, her eyes wide and apprehensive, her lips trembling a little as she said:

"Please . . please . . do not make me . . tell you! If I . . d . . do . . I am sure you will . . think I have been . . foolish in . . running away . . and that I must do as I have . . been told."

She made a sound that was like a sob before she added:

"If I have to . . do that . . I swear to you . . I will throw myself into the . . sea . . and drown first!"

She spoke so frantically and at the same time so violently that the Marquis stared at her in astonishment.

She had been so admirably controlled up until now.

He could hardly believe that she was the same girl who had prevented herself from crying when she found her Aunt was dead.

Very gently, so as not to frighten her more than she was already, he put his hand over hers which were clasped together.

"Now listen, Lela," he said. "I would not make you do anything you do not want to do, and certainly not something that makes you as upset as you are at this moment."

She stared at him, her eyes shining with unshed tears.

"Do you . . do you . . mean that?" she asked in a voice that seemed to be strangled in her throat.

"I swear it," he answered, "and I will only try to help you in the way you want to be helped."

She gave a little gasp and put her head down so that for a moment her face rested against his hand which covered hers.

He could feel the softness of her lips but knew she was not kissing him, but thinking of his hand as being a part of his kindness.

She thought of him, he felt, as a rock of protection, a superhuman being who had come to her rescue.

He had no idea how he knew this.

Yet he was aware it was so, and that she was different from any other woman he had ever known.

Then, as if she felt he was waiting, she said in a very small voice he could hardly hear:

"I . . I ran away because my . . Stepfather who is my Guardian . . has told me to . . m . . marry a man I have only seen . . twice who is . . old and . . horrible!"

Lela raised her eyes to his face, and the Marquis could feel her hands trembling beneath his.

He could feel too her breasts that were touching his leg were almost moving tumultuously.

"And who is your Stepfather?" he asked.

132

He thought for a moment she was not going to answer him. Then she said in the same small voice:

"H . . his name . . Sir Robert . . Lawson . . and he lives at The Towers near Great Milton in Oxfordshire."

She thought as she spoke that if the Marquis turned against her now she was finished.

If he sent her back she really would die.

"I have heard of him because he owns a number of race-horses," the Marquis said. "But he has no right to make you marry somebody you dislike."

"He has . . made up . . his mind . . and he is . . determined I shall . . do so," Lela whispered.

"In that case, until he changes it, you must continue to stay in hiding," the Marquis said.

Lela gave a cry and raised her head.

"Do you mean that . . do you really . . mean it? You will not . . make me go . . back to . . him?"

"No, of course not!" the Marquis said. "How can you imagine I would do anything so cruel?"

"Oh . . thank you . . thank you . . I know because my Stepfather is rich and Mr. Hopthorne also is wealthy that . . everybody would . . I am lucky not to have to go on being . . poor! But I would rather . . live in a . . garret than m . . marry a man I . . do not . . l . . love!"

The Marquis thought there were few women in the Social World who would feel like that.

He could understand that Lela was far too sensitive to contemplate a loveless marriage, even if everything she touched was made of gold.

"You have no money of your own?" he asked quietly.

"We had . . nothing after Papa was . . killed," Lela answered. "I think it was only because Mama wanted . . me to be . . properly educated . . that she . . married Sir Robert."

She drew in her breath before she added:

"He was kind and generous when . . Mama was alive,

133

but now she is . . dead he is . . different . . quite different . . and as he is impressed by Mr. Hopthorne . . he is determined . . that I shall . . marry him!"

"Then it is certainly something that must be prevented," the Marquis said.

But as he spoke he was wondering how it would be possible for Lela to go on hiding indefinitely.

He was well aware, having heard the story, how difficult it was for any young girl to fight against her Guardian's decision.

He thought too that Lela was right in thinking that the majority of people, unlike himself would think that such a marriage was in her best interests.

They would be convinced that as she had no money and nothing but a pretty face to recommend her, she was exceedingly fortunate to be offered a rich husband.

Then he was aware that Lela was looking up at him as if he was Jupiter, King of the Gods, who solved all problems.

"You will . . help me? You . . really will . . help me?" she asked, and now there was a lilt in her voice.

"I swear to you I will do my best," the Marquis said, "but as you must realise, it is going to be difficult."

"All I . . want is to . . hide somewhere, where my Stepfather . . cannot find me," Lela said.

She hesitated before she went on:

"Nanny said . . perhaps you would have a . . cottage on your estate . . ?"

She looked up at the Marquis and said quickly:

"Only a very tiny one . . and I would not be any trouble . . or bother you in . . any way . . but I am sure just because . . you are there . . and it was your . . land . . I would . . feel safe and . . protected."

"It is certainly an idea," the Marquis said, "and something we will talk about, Lela, on our way to England."

He took his hand from hers and said:

"Now I think you should go to bed, and I want you to try and sleep peacefully. If you do not wake up until we are home I shall understand."

"I shall . . want to . . wake up when . . you come aboard," Lela said.

She rose slowly to her feet, making it a very graceful movement.

The Marquis rose too, and put his arm round her shoulder as they walked towards the door of the Saloon.

"Now go to bed," he said again, "and do not worry. Leave everything to me."

"It is . . what I . . want to do," Lela whispered, "and thank you . . thank you for being so . . so wonderful!"

She was so lovely as she did so, and at the same time so young and helpless, that the Marquis's arm instinctively tightened around her.

"I am sure everything will be all right," he said.

Without thinking, he bent and kissed her cheek.

As he did so he felt a tremor run through her, and felt a surprising reaction within himself.

Then quickly, because he thought he had been indiscreet, he released her and walked out on deck.

"Goodnight, Lela," he said. "I will see you tomorrow."

As he spoke he hurried down the gangplank and onto the side of the canal.

As he walked away on the other side of the trees he was aware that she was watching him.

Instinctively he hurried his step – running away, he thought, not from Lela, but from his own feelings.

Chapter Seven

Lela lay in bed thinking of the Marquis and wondering if he had enjoyed himself with the *Vicomtesse* after she had left.

He had been so kind and understanding when she told him her secret, that she felt as if he had left a warm glow burning inside her.

"He is . . wonderful!" she whispered.

Then at the thought that they were going back to England tomorrow, she felt frightened.

Although he might find her somewhere to live, she would never see him again.

"I will never . . never . . forget him!" she thought, and remembered how he had kissed her cheek.

The feeling it had given her was very strange.

It was almost like a shower of stars streaking through her body, and it was something she had never known before.

Quite unexpectedly she found herself thinking that she would like him to kiss her on the lips.

When Mr. Hopthorne had tried to do that, it had revolted her and made her feel it would be something disgusting and horrible.

But she thought that Marquis's kiss would be very different, and something she would remember when she could no longer see him.

She wondered if he wanted to kiss the *Vicomtesse* and

136

was certain from the way the Frenchwoman behaved that she would welcome it.

She remembered how the Marquis sat next to the *Vicomtesse* on the sofa and how she whispered to him in her seductive voice.

Suddenly Lela began to cry.

The Marquis slowed his pace as he drew nearer to the Count's house.

He was thinking of Lela and her problem and wondering what he could possibly do about it.

He was well aware that if he gave her a cottage on his estate, as she had suggested, it would only be a question of time before people inferred that she was his mistress.

That was something he knew would never enter her mind.

But if he had to protect her from other men, he also had to protect her reputation against the slur of being involved with him.

"What can I do?" he asked himself over and over again. "What the devil can I do?"

He went into the Sitting-Room where the *Vicomtesse* in his absence was flirting with the Count.

"Have you seen that child off to bed?" she asked. "I am afraid you will find her rather a tiresome passenger on your voyage to England. Women invariably suffer from *mal-de-mer*."

The Marquis did not answer, being acutely aware that the *Vicomtesse* was being "catty".

It was something he most disliked, especially, he found himself thinking, where it concerned Lela.

Because he had no intention of answering what the *Vicomtesse* had said, he walked to the grog-tray in the corner of the room saying as he did so:

"May I help myself to a drink, Hans?"

"Of course!" the Count replied. "There is champagne or anything else you prefer."

"I am just thirsty," the Marquis answered, and poured himself a glass of water.

"Come and sit down," the *Vicomtesse* said patting the seat beside her, "and tell me about yourself."

"As a matter of fact," the Marquis replied in his most lofty voice, "I am going to say goodnight, as I intend to leave early tomorrow morning. I wish to have a word with my Captain before he goes to his cabin."

The *Vicomtesse* gave a little cry of protest, but the Count, who realised his friend genuinely did wish to leave, rose to his feet.

"You know, Carew, how sorry I am that you are leaving so soon," he said, "but you must admit I have provided you with some very fine paintings."

"I am deeply grateful," the Marquis replied, "and I suggest that the next time His Majesty comes to Kyne you join my party and explain to him how clever you have been!"

The Count laughed.

"I am very grateful for your suggestion. At the same time, I would rather come when you are alone. I see enough pictures in Holland, and all I want is to ride your magnificent horses."

The Marquis smiled.

"They are always at your disposal."

"Horses! Horses!" the *Vicomtesse* exclaimed. "Do Englishmen never speak of anything else?"

She was speaking somewhat petulantly.

She was annoyed that the Marquis was leaving her, and knew she had failed in her intention of enslaving him.

The Marquis raised her hand perfunctorily to his lips.

"Goodbye *Madame*, it has been a very great pleasure to meet you."

He and Hans moved towards the door.

When they were outside in the hall the Count said:

"Your little protégée is the most beautiful thing I have seen in years! I am prepared to offer the Rijks for her, if you are interested."

The Marquis laughed.

"She is not mine, and she has very definite ideas of her own as to what sort of man she wishes to marry."

"You are insulting me!" the Count complained.

Then he put his arm through the Marquis's and said:

"As I know of old, Carew, it is no use challenging you, You always win the race whether it concerns horses or women!"

"Now that is a compliment I do appreciate!" the Marquis said jokingly.

They were both laughing as he went down the steps and started to walk back to the yacht.

The canal looked very romantic with the lights from the road and the houseboats reflected on the water.

The Marquis found himself thinking with the stars overheard it was a fitting background from Lela.

Then he decided he had made a mistake in kissing her cheek.

He was annoyingly aware of the feelings it had evoked in him and that a quiver had run through her.

"She looks on me as a father-figure!" he told himself defiantly.

Yet as he walked up the gangplank he knew, however much he might deny it, that he was looking forward to the voyage because she would be with him.

They did not leave as early as the Marquis had intended.

But it was still too early for the Count to come and see them off.

They steamed out through the great port in which Amsterdam had once been no more than a small fishing village.

The Marquis was on the bridge as the *Heron* passed the warehouses, the dockyards and the small wharfs belonging to the grain, the timber, the oil and coal merchants.

They reached the entrance to the Noordzee Kanaal.

As soon as the *Heron* started down it the Marquis decided he was bored with large locks.

He went to the Saloon where breakfast was ready for him, but there was no sign of Lela.

He thought, after all she had passed through the previous day, it was a good thing for her to sleep.

It was not until they were out in the open sea that she came on deck.

Although it was of course ridiculous, he thought that she was looking even more lovely than he remembered.

Feeling perturbed by such thoughts occurring to him, he said mockingly:

'I began to think you were Mrs. Rip van Winkle, or else by mistake, I had left Holland without you!"

"I am ashamed of sleeping for so long," she answered, "but it is very exciting to be at sea in such a lovely yacht!"

"It is certainly a fine day," he said absent-mindedly.

As she looked eagerly at the sunkissed waves, she might, he thought, have been a sprite or a mermaid who had come abroad to bemuse mankind.

Then because he was angry with himself for being so imaginative he walked into the Saloon and she followed him.

"As there is a distinct swell," he said, "it would be best to sit here, or do you feel seasick?"

"I was not in the least sick when we came to Holland," she replied, "although Nanny only survived the voyage by drinking endless cups of tea, which she is doing again now!"

"But you feel no need for that?" the Marquis asked.

140

"I am just happy to be able to sit and talk to you," Lela said simply.

He contrasted the way she spoke with the manner in which the *Vicomtesse* would have uttered exactly the same words.

Before he could reply, Lela was asking him intelligent questions about the yacht.

She also wanted to know how much faster the crossing would be than if she travelled by the ordinary Steamer.

Afterwards they had luncheon and talked of everything except her destination when they arrived in England.

Finally she said a little hesitatingly:

"Have you . . thought, My Lord . . where I can . . hide when we reach England?"

"I have been giving the matter a lot of consideration," the Marquis replied, "and the only thing I can think of for the moment is that I speak to a member of my family, in fact my Aunt, who lives very quietly since she is a widow and could be trusted with your problem."

"Does your Aunt . . live in London?" Lela asked.

The Marquis nodded.

"Then she may . . perhaps have . . heard of my Stepfather . . or her . . friends may have seen him on a racecourse."

It was something the Marquis had thought of himself, and he said:

"There will be difficulties wherever you go."

"Perhaps I should have . . stayed in Holland," Lela said as if she was thinking to herself, "but as I could not . . now stay with Aunt Edith . . it would be . . expensive."

"Have you no money?" the Marquis enquired.

Lela blushed and looked away from him.

"I have . . enough," she said, "if we are . . careful."

"I want to know exactly how much," he persisted.

"My Stepfather . . gave me £50 to spend on . . things

141

for my . . trousseau," Lela faltered, "but of course . . we spent some of it . . in going . . to Holland."

"Fifty pounds!" the Marquis exclaimed. "How long, you foolish child, do you think . . that will . . last you?"

"Perhaps I could . . find something . . to do," Lela murmured.

The Marquis did not reply and after a moment she went on without thinking:

"I can paint . . quite well . . and I might be able to . . sell my pictures."

The Marquis gave a sudden exclamation.

"Good Heavens! I absolutely forgot!"

"Forgot what?" Lela asked.

"The sketch you brought me by Vermeer. The Count put it into a cupboard when the Dealers arrived so that they would not see it, and I never thought about it again!"

Lela was suddenly very still. Then she said:

"I have . . something to . . tell you . . My Lord!"

"What is it?" the Marquis asked.

He saw she was clasping her hands together in a gesture which he knew meant she was perturbed.

He saw also she had suddenly gone very pale, and the frightened look was back in her eyes.

"Do not worry," he said. "Count Hans will send the sketch on to me as soon as he realises I have left without it."

"It is . . not that," Lela said, "but it is . . something which . . may make you . . angry."

The Marquis looked at her, wondering what she was going to say.

After a moment in a small voice he could hardly hear, Lela said:

"The sketch is a . . f . . fake!"

"A fake?"

The Marquis's voice was louder than he intended.

"What do you mean – it is a fake?"

142

"I . . I . . p . . painted it."

For a moment he could only stare at her in sheer astonishment.

"*You* painted it? What are you saying?" he asked. "How can you have painted it?"

"I was . . painting a copy of the Vermeer for Aunt Edith because she could not . . go to the Mauritshuis herself to . . see it . . and a man . . spoke to me . ."

"What man? Who was he?"

"It was . . Mr. Nijsted . . a Dealer . . and he said . . if I took it to you . . and pretended it was . . a sketch by . . Vermeer . . for his portrait . . the money you would . . give me . . for it would . . pay for . . Aunt Edith's operation."

The words came jerkily from between her lips.

She was vividly aware that the Marquis was staring at her, a scowl between his eyes.

"So you brought the sketch to me," he said "and deliberately lied!"

"I . . I knew it was . . wrong . ."

"Wrong?" the Marquis shouted the word. "Is there no woman in the world who is not treacherous and a liar? Dammit, I trusted you!"

He spoke so violently that Lela felt the tears come into her eyes.

Then as he finished speaking, the Marquis rose from his chair and walked to the porthole to look out to sea.

He stood with his back to her, but his voice still seemed to be reverberating round the Saloon.

As the tears poured down Lela's face she slipped out through the door and down the companionway to her own cabin.

She thought miserably that now the Marquis would have nothing more to do with her.

She knew that he despised her.

Tears blinded her eyes as she groped her way across the cabin.

It flashed through her mind that perhaps the best thing she could do would be to fling herself into the sea.

Then all her troubles would be over.

She was aware of the hopeless position she was in without the sanctuary she had found with her Aunt.

She was without money, and now without the Marquis to help her.

She knew it was only a question of time before she and Nanny would have to return to her Stepfather before they starved.

He would then force her to marry Mr. Hopthorne, and after that there would be no escape.

"I shall . . have to . . die . . Papa," she said to her father.

She wondered how she could slip into the sea without anybody aboard the yacht being aware of it, and saving her from drowning.

She moved across her cabin towards a porthole.

Her movement was unsteady because as they neared the shores of England the sea had grown rougher, and the wind was making the waves tempestuous.

She reached the porthole and tried to look out.

She could however see nothing but a blur because of the tears that were still running down her cheeks.

"I love him . . I love . . him!" she whispered, "and now . . he will never . . speak to me . . again!"

Everything seemed hopeless and her feeling of misery was overwhelming.

She could only stand holding onto the top of a bookcase for support, vainly trying to see outside. Suddenly there was a resounding crash like an explosion.

The heavy window of the porthole swung open and caught Lela a violent blow to the side of her head.

She fell to the floor as if pole-axed and knew no more.

The Marquis had stood for some time looking out to sea, the feeling of fury within him gradually subsiding.

He could hardly believe it possible that Lela, who had seemed so sweet, pure and innocent, should have tried to deceive him.

It was the same way that Lady Burton and Dolly Leslie had tried to do.

They had driven him from England.

Now, on his return journey, he found for the third time a woman had decided to make a fool of him.

"Damn her! Damn all women!" he swore beneath his breath.

Then he was suddenly ashamed of himself.

It was very unlike him to lose his self-control.

He could only attribute it to the fact that, because Lela was so small and so helpless, he had wanted to protect and look after her.

Now that he began to breathe more easily his anger was abating.

He could understand how she had been tempted by a very shrewd Picture Dealer.

Hans had told him a lot about them and the different ways in which they extracted money from unsuspecting customers.

It was very much the same, he supposed, when it concerned the sale of horses.

Unscrupulous Dealers would extol an inferior animal, fake its pedigree, and find some 'Greenhorn' to pay an exorbitant sum for a horse that was worth no more than a quarter of the price.

As he now thought it over, he could understand that Lela had been desperately anxious to find the money for her Aunt's operation.

It was the Dealer who had persuaded her to deceive him.

Seeing how lovely she was, he was sure too that Nijsted

would think he was more likely to pay a large sum of money for the sketch than if a Dealer had brought it to him.

Nijsted would undoubtedly expect to receive at least half of anything that he paid for it.

The Marquis was glad that when the man realised Lela had left Amsterdam he would know he had lost a fat commission.

With an effort, he turned round, saying as he did so:

"I am sorry, Lela, that I swore at you!"

As he spoke he saw that the Saloon was empty and Lela had gone.

He wondered if he should follow her.

Suddenly there was a loud noise, the whole yacht quivered, and he realised they had hit something.

He thought it must be a rock.

As he ran out of the Saloon to investigate, the Mate came running down the deck from the bridge.

Before the Marquis could speak he said:

"A trawler swung into us, M'Lord, and hit us starboard amidship. I'm going below to see if it's damaged the Lady's cabin."

"I will do that," the Marquis said sharply.

He hurried down the companionway and along the passage.

He opened the door of Lela's cabin and saw the impact of the trawler had forced open the porthole.

The sea was pouring in every time the yacht rolled.

Lela was lying on the floor, soaked in sea water.

The Marquis bent down to pick her up, he realised that when the window of the porthole burst open it had struck her on her temple, which was bleeding.

As he lifted her in his arms, like a knife-thrust in his heart he thought she was dead.

He knew then that he loved her as he had never loved a woman before.

Lela came back to consciousness through a long, dark tunnel which had a faint light at the end of it.

She thought she must have been asleep for a very long time, and it was an effort to open her eyes.

As she did so, she remembered she was in the yacht and the Marquis was angry with her.

Then she saw there was a canopy over her head which she had not seen before, and as gradually she focused her eyes she saw that she was in a large room.

As she gave a little murmur of surprise, Nanny rose from where she was sitting at the side of the window and came to the bedside.

"Are you awake, Dearie?" she asked.

Lela wanted to put out a hand to hold onto Nanny, but it was too much of an effort.

"Where . . am . . I?" she whispered.

"You're quite safe, and everything's all right."

"Wh . . what . . h . . happened?"

"You got hurt on the yacht, but go to sleep, I'll tell you all about it tomorrow."

Lela wanted to know now, but felt too tired to say so.

She closed her eyes, and knew nothing more.

"There! You look quite yourself, except for that nasty bruise on your forehead!" Nanny exclaimed.

"Does it look very ugly?" Lela asked.

"It's black, as if you've been in the wars!" Nanny replied. "But the Doctor says it'll soon disappear, and there's no reason for there to be even a scar!"

Lela gave a sigh of relief.

It would have been much worse, she thought, if the porthole window, which she now realised had hit her, had knocked out her teeth, or broken her nose.

Then as Nanny tidied the bed and picked up the luncheon-tray to take it from the room, Lela asked:

"Is His Lordship upset that we have . . stayed here for so . . long?"

"He's been kindness itself," Nanny said, "and his Aunt who is staying here to chaperon you, is as nice and kind as your mother, and I can't say fairer than that!"

There was a note of satisfaction in Nanny's voice.

Lela knew that she was comfortable and being supplied with good food and plenty of strong tea.

Nanny had reached the door when she asked:

"How . . long have we . . been here?"

"This is the fourth day," Nanny said, "and as far as I'm concerned, I'm in no hurry to leave!"

She went out and shut the door, and Lela smiled to herself.

It was certainly very different from having to hide in some sordid little Lodging-House which was all they could have afforded.

She could remember nothing of being brought from the yacht, which had managed, despite the damage done by the trawler, to reach Greenwich.

"His Lordship carried you to his carriage," Nanny had told her, "and you lay on the back-seat while he and I sat on the small one."

"He must have . . disliked that," Lela thought, but she did not say so aloud.

A very important Doctor, who was in attendance on the King, had come to see her.

He had called every day, but this morning he had said:

"You are recovering from your accident far quicker than I expected, but you are still to rest. I shall not come tomorrow, unless His Lordship sends for me, but the day after."

"Thank you very much for all you have done," Lela said.

He smiled at her before he replied:

"You are quite the most beautiful patient I have ever

had, and I can assure you I have had quite a number of them!"

She blushed at the compliment, and he smiled again as he said:

"Do not worry. In a week or so you will be as good as new! However, I should be careful of portholes the next time you travel in a yacht!"

He had not waited for her answer, but hurried away, making it very clear that he was an exceedingly busy man.

Now she was alone, Lela wondered if she would ever see the Marquis.

She wanted to ask about him, but had been too shy to enquire even from Nanny if he was in the house.

If he was, she was sure that he would be entertaining his smart friends.

He would never give a thought to his unwanted guest with whom he was still angry.

"Why was I not brave enough to reject Mr. Nijsted from the very beginning?" she asked herself despairingly.

Then she knew that if she had done so, she would never have met the Marquis.

However angry he might be, even if she had to leave his house without seeing him, she knew she would be grateful for having known him.

Nor would she ever forget the kiss he had given her on her cheek.

She knew now that what she had felt when he did so was love.

It was the love that was like the sunshine and the stars, the beauty she had found in the Hague and in Vermeer's portrait.

And yet it was much more than that.

It was a feeling that made her want to worship the Marquis because he was so wonderful.

That he no longer trusted her was like being thrown out of Heaven, as the Archangel Lucifer had been.

She was falling down into Hell.

"I love him . . I love him!" she told herself as she had done a thousand times already, and felt the tears come into her eyes.

There was a knock on the door.

Then without waiting for her to answer it, somebody opened the door and came in.

She thought it would be one of the maids and turned her head aside as she wiped her eyes so that they would not see she had been crying.

Then as somebody came to the bedside she gave a little gasp when she saw it was the Marquis.

"Sir William has told me that you are now allowed visitors," he said, "so I have come to see you."

Because it was so exciting to see him and something she had not expected, Lela's voice died in her throat.

Her blue eyes were shining not only with her tears, but because he was there.

He was looking, she thought, even more handsome, more wonderful than he had ever been before.

For a moment they just looked at each other.

Then the Marquis sat down on the side of the bed.

"I am desperately sorry this happened to you," he said.

"Are you . . still . . angry with me?" Lela whispered.

It was such a vital question that she could not pay attention to anything else the Marquis was saying.

She had to know his answer.

He reached out his hand and took hers, and she felt herself quiver because he was touching her.

"You have to forgive me," he said. "I have been very ashamed of myself for shouting at you, and for what I said."

"I have been . . wishing and wishing," Lela murmured, "that I had not . . listened to Mr Nijsted . . but then . . if I had not done so . . I would never have . . met you."

The Marquis's hand tightened on hers.

150

"Are you perhaps glad you did?"

"So . . very . . very glad."

She looked up at him and there seemed to be no need for words.

Something was being said between them that filled the whole room with light.

"You are not in pain?" the Marquis asked as if he forced the words to his lips.

He looked as he spoke at the livid bruise on her temple which Sir William had said would heal quicker without a bandage.

"Is it . . so very . . ugly?" Lela enquired.

"You look beautiful," the Marquis answered, "so beautiful Lela, that I cannot bear to think of you being hurt or injured, or having anything happen to you that might be ugly or frightening."

Lela thought he was referring to the fact that she had to hide somewhere, and that she would soon have to leave his house.

Her fingers tightened on his for a moment before she said, looking away from him:

"I . . I know it is an . . imposition for . . Nanny and me to be . . here . . and as soon as I am . . allowed to get up . . we will . . go away."

"And where will you go to?"

He saw the terror come into her eyes.

He knew without her telling him that she was feeling she would eventually, if not at once, have to return to her Stepfather.

Her lips trembled before she said in a voice which sounded brave:

"I . . I shall . . find somewhere . . I do not . . want to be a . . bother to you."

"Do you really think I would let you go without being sure you would be safe," the Marquis said, "and that no one could hurt or upset you?"

There was a note in his voice which seemed to vibrate into her breast.

It gave her the same warm feeling she had known once before.

"I expect I shall be . . all right."

"I want to ask you a question," the Marquis said in a different tone, "and I want you, Lela to promise me that you will tell the truth."

She thought he was not trusting her again, and she said quickly:

"I promise . . I will . . tell you the . . truth and never . . never lie to . . you again!"

She thought he would not believe her and she went on:

"I swear . . to you . . I never lie. It was only to . . save Aunt Edith that I . . pretended the . . picture was by Vermeer. Forgive me . . please . . please . . forgive me!"

She was pleading with all her heart.

Then as she did so she realised that the Marquis had moved closer to her, and his face was not very far from hers.

"I want you to answer a question," he said in his deep voice. "Tell me truthfully, Lela, what you feel about me."

"I . . I think you are wonderful! No man could . . have been so . . kind and . . understanding . ."

"Forget that," the Marquis interrupted. "Just go on with what you were saying about me."

"What can . . I say?" Lela asked. "Except that . ."

She stopped.

"I want to hear the end of that sentence," the Marquis said very quietly.

"It is . . something I . . cannot say!"

"Why not?"

"Because you . . will not . . want to . . hear it . . and . . you might . . laugh at me."

"I would never laugh at you! I have never laughed at

anything you have told me," the Marquis said. "Tell me, Lela, tell me the truth, as you promised to do."

She looked into his eyes and they were very close to hers.

Then as if some other voice was speaking instead of her own, she murmured almost beneath her breath:

"I . . . I love . . . you!"

"As I love you!" the Marquis said.

Then his lips were on hers, and Lela felt the starlight running through her body as it had before.

He kissed her at first very gently, as if she was infinitely precious and he was afraid of frightening her.

He felt the softness, sweetness and innocence of her lips.

Then he was aware that the ecstasy she felt was echoed within himself, his kiss became more demanding, more possessive.

He pressed her gently back against the pillows, and kissed her until they were both breathless.

Only when he raised his head did Lela say in a rapt little voice:

"I . . . love . . . you! I . . . love . . . you!"

Then as he did not speak she asked anxiously:

"You . . . you did say you loved me . . . you are not . . . angry?"

"I adore you! I was only angry because I could not imagine you doing anything wrong or anything that would hurt me."

"Will . . . you . . . forgive . . . me?"

"There is nothing to forgive," he said, "except of course if you want to make reparation, there is something you can do."

"What is . . . that?"

"Marry me as quickly as possible," the Marquis said, "for, my darling, I cannot live without you!"

Her face seemed transfigured, her eyes were shining as they looked into his.

"Are you . . . are you really . . . asking me to be . . . your wife?"

"I thought I hated women. I was determined not to marry for many years!" the Marquis said. "But now I cannot wait! We will be married as soon as I can get a Special Licence."

Lela suddenly realised that once she was married there would be nothing her Stepfather could do about it.

Yet because she was still afraid she said:

"You do . . . not have to . . . get permission from my . . . Guardian?"

"I am asking no one's permission!" the Marquis replied. "We are going to be married quickly, and secretly. Once you are my wife if your Stepfather tries to suggest I am not a suitable husband, he will merely look foolish!"

There was no need for the Marquis to put it into words that Sir Robert would be exceedingly impressed by him.

He could hardly claim that Mr. Hopthorne was a better "catch".

Lela put out her hand to hold onto the Marquis saying:

"Are you . . . quite sure . . . this is true . . . and I am not dreaming?"

"It is real and our love is real," the Marquis answered.

Lela hid her face against him.

"You do . . . not think . . . I am . . . a fake?"

The Marquis smiled, and his eyes were very tender.

"You are real, my precious one."

"You are . . . quite . . . quite . . . sure?"

"My heart speaks to your heart and your lips speak to my lips, and everything about you is mine – and perfect."

Lela made a little sound of joy which was like the song of the birds.

"I want . . . to be . . . yours," she murmured.

154

"And God knows I want you," the Marquis answered. "I am afraid to let you out of my sight in case I lose you."

He put his fingers under her chin and turned her face up to him.

He looked at her for a long moment until her eyelashes fluttered because she felt shy.

"Why do I want pictures, whoever painted them, when I have you?" he asked. "You are more beautiful, my darling, than anything an Artist has ever portrayed on canvas."

"That is . . . what I want you to think," Lela answered, "and . . . please . . . please . . . just in case . . . somebody lures you away from me . . . let us get married . . . as you said . . . very quickly!"

The Marquis knew she was thinking of the *Vicomtesse*.

"Do you really think anybody could take me from you?" he asked. "My lovely one, I have been looking for you all my life, but thought it impossible to find you! When you appeared looking so unbelievably adorable, you turned my whole world upside-down!"

"Please . . . help me to go on . . . doing that," Lela said, "and your world is so . . . exciting . . . like you . . . that whatever . . . difficulties we face . . . I shall be . . . thrilled to . . . be in . . . it!"

The Marquis laughed and kissed her again.

Only when the whole room had revolved dizzily and the sunshine seemed to be burning within them both did the Marquis say:

"I must leave you now my darling. I have a lot of plans to make, and most important of all I must obtain a Special Licence. Do you think you will feel well enough to marry me the day after tomorrow?"

"I am well enough . . . now!" Lela said. "Except that I am afraid I look . . . ugly for you!"

"Now you are fishing for compliments," the Marquis said. "I know, my precious one, that I cannot wait one more day, or one more hour than is absolutely necessary. We will be married in my Private Chapel at Kyne, which is where we will start our honeymoon."

Lela's eyes told him how excited she was at the idea.

Then as he would have risen from the bed she put out her hands to hold onto him.

"There is . . . one thing I . . . ought to ask you."

"What is that?" the Marquis enquired.

"Do you really think," she said slowly, "that you should . . . marry me? I am sure . . . I am not . . . important enough and . . . your family will disapprove."

The Marquis laughed, and it was a very happy sound.

"I am not concerned whether my family approve or do not approve," he said. "Actually they will be so delighted at my marrying at all, and especially to somebody as beautiful as you, that they will welcome you with open arms!"

Once again he put his hand under her chin.

"How can you be everything I want in one small person?" he asked. "As for being important enough, there are an enormous number of women in the world, but not one of them is as important to me as you."

Lela laughed because it sounded so funny.

Then she said seriously:

"I am sure . . . Papa helped me to . . . find you."

"He and your mother will bless our marriage, and we will live happily ever afterwards!" the Marquis said. "And there is nothing your Stepfather can do about it!"

Lela gave a little cry.

"Please . . . hurry and get . . . the Special Licence! I am so afraid that he will learn that I am here . . . and carry me away . . . before you can . . . save me!"

"I promise you, the doors are all locked and the servants have instructions to admit nobody except my friends and those I trust." the Marquis replied. "I have made it clear anyway as far as the world outside is concerned, that there is no one staying with me except for my Aunt."

"You think of . . . everything!" Lela said.

"I think of you, and for me there is nobody in the whole world except you!"

He kissed her again, fiercely and demandingly.

Then he kissed her eyes, her little straight nose, and the corners of her mouth.

Her lips were ready for him, but instead he kissed the softness of her neck arousing strange feelings she had never known before.

Shafts of sunlight were seeping through her and turning into little flames of fire.

Her body moved beneath the sheets and her breath came quickly between her parted lips.

The Marquis suddenly took his arms from her and sat up.

There was, Lela thought, a fire burning in his eyes.

"Take care of yourself, my very precious, very beautiful Wife-to-be," he said. "I will come back this evening and tell you how all my plans are progressing. Just get well, and very quickly, because I want you with me both by day and night."

There was a note of passion in the last word which made Lela blush.

Then as he went from the room, she put her hands together and shut her eyes.

"Thank You, God, thank You!" she prayed. "How can You have sent me such a wonderful, marvellous man? I promise that I will never . . . never . . . lie again!"

She drew in a deep breath before she added:

"I love . . . him! I love . . . him! Bless us so that I will always keep his love."

She was sure her prayer had been heard, for the room was filled with a light that was more vivid than the sun.

It was like their love – Divine and came from God.

OTHER BOOKS BY BARBARA CARTLAND

Romantic Novels, over 400, the most recently published being:

Love is Invincible
The Goddess of Love
An Adventure of Love
A Herb for Happiness
Only a Dream
Saved by Love
Little Tongues of Fire
A Chieftain Finds Love
The Lovely Liar
The Perfume of the Gods
A Knight in Paris
Revenge is Sweet
The Passionate Princess
Solita and the Spies
The Perfect Pearl
Love is a Maze
A Circus of Love
The Temple of Love
The Bargain Bride
The Haunted Heart

The Dream and the Glory (In aid of the St. John Ambulance Brigade)

Autobiographical and Biographical:
The Isthmus Years 1919–1939
The Years of Opportunity 1939–1945
I Search for Rainbows 1945–1976
We Danced All Night 1919–1929
Ronald Cartland (With a foreword by Sir Winston Churchill)
Polly – My Wonderful Mother
I Seek the Miraculous

Historical:
Bewitching Women
The Outrageous Queen (The Story of Queen Christina of Sweden)
The Scandalous Life of King Carol
The Private Life of Charles II
The Private Life of Elizabeth, Empress of Austria
Josephine, Empress of France
Diane de Poitiers

Metternich – The Passionate Diplomat
Royal Jewels
Royal Lovers
Royal Eccentrics

Sociology:
You in the Home
The Fascinating Forties
Marriage for Moderns
Be Vivid, Be Vital
Love, Life and Sex
Vitamins for Vitality
Husbands and Wives
Men are Wonderful
Keep Young and Beautiful by Barbara Cartland and Elinor Glyn
Etiquette for Love and Romance
Barbara Cartland's Book of Health
Etiquette
The Many Facets of Love
Sex and the Teenager
The Book of Charm
Living Together
The Youth Secret
The Magic of Honey
The Book of Beauty and Healing

Cookery:
Barbara Cartland's Health Food Cookery Book
Food for Love
Magic of Honey Cookbook
Recipes for Lovers
The Romance of Food

Editor of:
"The Common Problem" by Ronald Cartland (with a preface by The
Rt. Hon. The Earl of Selborne, P.C.)
Barbara Cartland's Library of Love
Library of Ancient Wisdom
"Written with Love" Passionate love letters selected by Barbara
Cartland

Drama:
Blood Money
French Dressing

Philosophy:
Touch the Stars

Radio Operetta:
The Rose and the Violet (Music by Mark Lubbock) Performed in 1942.

Radio Plays:
The Caged Bird: An episode in the life of Elizabeth Empress of Austria
Performed in 1957.

General:
Barbara Cartland's Book of Useless Information with a Foreword by
the Earl Mountbatten of Burma.
(In aid of the United World Colleges)
Love and Lovers (Picture Book)
The Light of Love (Prayer Book)
Barbara Cartland's Scrapbook
(In aid of the Royal Photographic Museum)
Romantic Royal Marriages
Barbara Cartland's Book of Celebrities
Getting Older, Growing Younger

Verse:
Lines on Life and Love

Music:
An Album of Love Songs sung with the Royal Philharmonic Orchestra.

Film:
A Hazard of Hearts
The Lady and the Highwayman
A Ghost in Monte Carlo

Cartoons:
Barbara Cartland Romances (Book of Cartoons) has recently been published in the U.S.A., Great Britain, and other parts of the world.

Children:
A Children's Pop-Up Book: "Princess to the Rescue"

Videos:
A Hazard of Hearts
The Lady and the Highwayman
A Ghost in Monte Carlo